D0883742

BARBARA JORDAN

BARBARA JORDAN by

JAMES HASKINS

The Dial Press / New York

LIBRARY
WESTERN OREGON STATE COLLEGE
MONMOUTH, OREGON 97361

JUV.
E
840.8
.J62
H34
1977

#921
J.

Copyright © 1977 by James Haskins
All rights reserved. No part of this book may be reproduced
in any form or by any means without the prior written permission
of the publisher, excepting brief quotes used in connection with
reviews written specifically for inclusion in a magazine or newspaper.
Printed in the United States of America · First Printing
Typography by Denise Cronin Neary

Excerpt from *Adam by Adam* by Adam Clayton Powell, Jr.
published by The Dial Press.

Library of Congress Cataloging in Publication Data
Haskins, James, 1941-Barbara Jordan.
Bibliography: p. Includes index.
Summary: A biography of the Congresswoman from Texas, the first
black woman ever to be elected to that office from the South.
1. Jordan, Barbara, 1936-   —Juvenile literature.
2. Legislators—United States—Biography—Juvenile literature.
[1. Jordan, Barbara, 1936-   2. Legislators.
3. Afro-Americans—Biography] I. Title.
E840.8.J62H36   328.73′092′4 [B] [92]   77-71522
ISBN 0-8037-0452-6

I am grateful to Susan Fener for her research work, and to Mary Ellen Arrington, who typed the manuscript drafts. A special thanks to Kathy Benson.

BARBARA JORDAN

If there are any patriots left, I am one.

BARBARA JORDAN

1 Early Years

It was hot outside on that late July afternoon in Washington, D.C., and inside the chambers of the House Judiciary Committee the climate was almost subtropical. The television-camera strobe lights were hot, and the myriad video equipment radiated additional heat, as did the bodies of the people who packed the room. Congressional aides and spectators vied for space and view with members of the media—reporters from television, radio, and newspapers; newspaper photographers; television camera and audio men. On a raised, two-tiered platform at the front of the room sat the thirty-eight men and women of the House Judiciary Committee, trying to conduct the business at hand in a solemn, no-nonsense manner. The task was extremely difficult. Despite the intention of most of the members to conduct their historic business as decorously as possible, this was no ordinary committee hearing. The House Judiciary Committee hearings on the impeachment of President Richard M. Nixon were a media event.

As seen through the eyes of the television cameras, each member of the House Judiciary Committee took on a particular personality, like actors in a dramatic series. The American public could understand the party, geographic, racial, and sexual lines that were drawn within the committee. Republicans and southern Democrats seemed to be sympathetic to the president. Northern Democrats, blacks, and women seemed to be against him. But within these groupings each member was a unique personality, and many seemed "made" for television: William L. Hungate, Democrat of Missouri, with his folksy wisdom and humor; strident Charles Sandman, Republican of New Jersey; earnest Tom Railsback, Republican of Illinois.

Anyone watching the proceedings closely, day in and day out, learned what to expect from most of these people. They would state and restate their opinions, each in his or her own particular way, some quietly, some harshly. Each would invoke the Constitution, for it was a constitutional question they were addressing in deciding whether or not to recommend impeachment, and

*The House Judiciary Committee assembles to begin
debate on the possible impeachment of President Nixon.
Barbara Jordan is second from left.*

each would claim that the Constitution supported his or her opinion. After a time the word *Constitution* became almost meaningless. But on July 25, 1974, when "the gentlelady from Texas," as Chairman Peter Rodino called Congresswoman Barbara Jordan, faced the television cameras and began to speak, the concepts of the Constitution took on a new meaning, and in this era of media events, she became a media personality.

" 'We, the people,' " she began in her resonant voice, "—it is a very eloquent beginning. But when the Constitution of the United States was completed on the 17th of September in 1787, I was not included in that 'We, the people.' I felt for many years that somehow George Washington and Alexander Hamilton just left me out by mistake. . . ."

There was no humor in that beginning of her speech. Barbara Jordan is black. And her statement that for many years she thought she'd been "just left out by mistake" rang true. Most American parents stress to their children the importance of being Americans; but after a time, black and other minority children learn that while they are American-born, they are not the same sort of American as white children. It's very hard for children to accept being different through no fault of their own. "Maybe someone just forgot us," they decide.

Barbara Charline Jordan was born at a time and in a place where only children could entertain such an idea. Black adults in Houston, Texas, in the 1930s understood that they were second-class Americans and had learned to live with that knowledge. They lived and worked knowing that they were limited not only by social customs but by actual laws. They had to use "colored" restrooms and water fountains, which were never as plentiful or accessible as those reserved for whites. When they rode on public buses they had to sit in the back, and if the bus was crowded they were expected to give up their seats to whites. They lived in segregated housing and had to send their children to segregated schools. In theory, they possessed the right to vote to change these conditions. But poll taxes and literacy tests and outright intimidation by whites prevented most of them from going to the polls to change the discriminatory laws. Their influence was so slight that they could not even get decent lighting for their streets.

In 1930 blacks made up 22 percent of the population of Houston, a city that existed as two separate societies connected only by economic necessity. The three main black areas—San Felipe near downtown, the southeast and the northeast parts of the city— seemed to exist only to serve the white areas, for the majority of the black people who lived in these areas earned whatever meager incomes they did earn in service to whites—as maids and nannies, as chauffeurs and yardmen and laundry workers. These blacks had to go to the white areas to work, but otherwise they avoided placing themselves in situations that were degrading to them—and almost every situation in which they found themselves in the white areas was degrading. If they went downtown to shop, they were served in the *back* of the store; if they were hungry, they had to walk blocks to find a cafeteria or restaurant that would serve them. The white sections were filled with perils for blacks, who could be stopped on any pretext by a policeman or accused of wrongdoing if they dared look a white person in the eye. So the blacks stayed out of the white areas as much as possible and kept to themselves in their segregated enclaves. There they might be poor and without legal or political influence, but at least they did not have to worry about walking on the "wrong" side of the street or looking in the "wrong" direction. And they kept their children in these enclaves as long as possible, to shield them from the brutal realities of the world outside. As long as they were so shielded, the black children of Houston had little idea of the larger world. It was possible to go for days without seeing a single white person other than a policeman. As Barbara Jordan recalls, "We were all black and we were all poor and we were all right there in one place. For us, the larger community didn't exist."

Barbara was born on February 21, 1936, the youngest of Benjamin and Arlyne Jordan's three children, all of whom were girls. Her father was a Baptist minister, with churches in the rural areas of Thompsons and Kendleton, and thus the Jordan family enjoyed a position of some respect in the Houston black community. The black church was one of the few areas where blacks controlled their own activities relatively free from white supervision; it was the hub of organization, cooperation, management, finance, and self-government in the black neighborhood. The black minister, therefore, was a combination social, moral, and political leader, and a major force in the community. Still, black churchgoers in rural parishes were not financially able to support their minister. To supplement his scanty income, Benjamin Jordan also worked as a warehouse clerk. The family lived in a modest frame house at 4910 Campbell Street surrounded by a small, well-kept green lawn. Inside, the furnishings were simple but adequate, just like those in the other houses on the street. "We were poor," says Barbara Jordan, "but so was everyone around us, so we didn't notice it. We were never hungry and we always had a place to stay."

Family life for the Jordans revolved around two basic areas—religion and music. God was ever-present, and though they did not have much money, they were secure in the belief that they were cared for and loved. Music, too, was ever-present. Both Benjamin and Arlyne Jordan sang and played musical instruments, and they encouraged the musical abilities of their daughters. Barbara's favorite instrument was the guitar.

Music was the chief source of pleasure in the Jordan family. Card playing, for example, was strictly forbidden, for Mr. Jordan considered it a sinful activity. "We were raised in the strictest Baptist sense," says Barbara, "—no drinking, smoking, or dancing." The girls were encouraged to read—all were familiar with the Bible at a very young age. Books on history were favored, and no novels or comic books were allowed.

Mr. Jordan was a strict disciplinarian, and much of the great self-control that Barbara Jordan exhibits is due to his influence. "I always had to keep the lid on, no matter how angry I got," she says. "It did not have to do with his being a minister; it was my respect for him as a person. I had great respect. It was unthinkable to have a hot exchange of words with him, for me or my mother or any of us. So one does develop quite a bit of control that way. I suppose the kids now would say that was not good."

While he was very strict, her father was also very supportive. His great loves, Barbara has said, were his family, his faith, and his language, in that order. As a grown man Benjamin Jordan was highly aware of the inequities that black people suffered in a predominantly white, segregated society, but to hear him speak to his young daughters, one would never have known it. They were told early and often that they could be anything they wanted to be as long as they were willing to work for it. And he told them, and showed them by example, that one's sense of dignity and self-worth is not derived from others but from oneself.

Today, when she speaks to groups of young people,

Barbara echoes her father's sentiments: "There is no obstacle in the path of young people who are poor or members of minority groups that hard work and thorough preparation cannot cure. Do not call for black power or green power. Call for brain power."

Benjamin Jordan demanded a considerable amount of brain power from his daughters. Intelligence is not subject to either discrimination or segregation: "No man can take away your brain," he would tell his children. And Benjamin Jordan expected not only intelligent thinking but also intelligent articulation of those thoughts. He loved the English language—the power of the precise word and its precise pronunciation. It was from her father that Barbara learned the speaking ability that has become her hallmark.

Barbara grew to be very much like her father, and in later years it was hard for the two to recall who was stricter with her—her father or Barbara herself. Barbara recalls, "I would bring home five A's and one B, and my father would say, 'Why do you have a B?' " But Benjamin Jordan used to remember report card time differently: "She was unhappy if she made less than a straight A average in school." Barbara was a competitive youngster, but her concern for grades was not just a matter of outdoing her classmates; it was a matter of living up to her own rigorous standards.

Partially because of her father's supportiveness, but mostly because of something in herself, Barbara needed little outside reinforcement of her sense of self-worth.

Serious, controlled, mature beyond her years, she had a natural dignity. Her father once said, "I realized when she was a little girl that Barbara was one of the rare ones."

As she grew older, Barbara Jordan began to understand that the world she knew—the black community, segregated black schools—was a very small, insular one and that beyond it was a large and not particularly friendly white world. She still did not have to deal with it personally very often, but she began to learn about it from books and from hearing people talk. In school she learned about slavery and studied the history of the United States. In the 1940s and early 1950s, when she was in grade school and high school, black Americans accommodated themselves to the discrimination and segregation they suffered from the larger white society. Black children heard little militant rhetoric, were not taught to feel bitterness about the hypocrisy of a so-called democracy in which a sizable minority group enjoyed few rights. Yet a bright and perceptive youngster like Barbara Jordan could not help noticing that the United States Constitution had been written and adopted without a single mention of *slavery*, *bondage*, or *Negro*. That fact troubled her. "Maybe," she sadly concluded, "they just forgot."

By the time she entered high school, Barbara had acquired a greater understanding of race relations in the United States. She had felt the sting of racist remarks and the sense of how unfair it was to be judged by the color of her skin rather than by her intelligence or her personality or her character. She had listened to her parents and other black adults talk about the lack of opportunities for black people and about the long list of civil and legal rights they did not have. She had come to realize that the framers of the Constitution had not forgotten her at all, that they had deliberately avoided mentioning black people. Why this was she could not be sure, but she suspected that the men who had written the document had recognized the hypocrisy of stating that "all men are created equal" and then including in that document mention of the very people who were not treated as equal. The framers of the laws in the southern United States in the mid-twentieth century were not so sensitive. Their laws clearly indicated their belief that only whites were created equal.

Barbara knew that as a black person the odds were against her. Further, she was a woman and not even possessed of the qualities that women have traditionally used to their advantage. As she told her homeroom teacher in high school, "I am big and black and fat and ugly, and I will never have a man problem." She had often heard adults say that a black person had to be twice as good as a white person in order to succeed. And yet all that daunted her not at all; she intended to succeed, and in a big way. "I always wanted to be something unusual," she says. "I never wanted to be run-of-the-mill. For a while I thought about being a pharmacist, but then I thought, whoever heard of an outstanding pharmacist?"

Her two older sisters, Bennie and Rose Mary, wanted to be music teachers. That was a realistic goal for young black women in Texas. But Barbara was more ambitious. She wanted to be something more. She just couldn't figure out what.

Avidly she read biographies of successful people; she particularly liked reading the life stories of presidents. There were many black people whose lives could serve as models—black people who had become famous or successful despite the strictures of white society. There was Frederick Douglass, who had been born in slavery and had escaped to the North to play a major role in the abolition movement. There was Booker T. Washington, who had been the chief spokesman for black people early in the twentieth century and who had founded Tuskegee Institute in Alabama. W. E. B. DuBois had graduated from Harvard University at a time when only a miniscule proportion of the black population even went to college, and had gone on to be a major black writer and intellectual. There were women too. Like Frederick Douglass, Harriet Tubman had been born in slavery and had escaped to the North. Her part in the fight against slavery had been different from Douglass's, but no less important. She became one of the most famous "conductors" on the Underground Railroad, risking her own safety over and over to lead hundreds of slaves to the North and freedom. A half century later, Mary McLeod Bethune also served as a role model for young black girls. As a young woman she had founded a school for black girls in Florida, which later became Bethune-Cookman College. During the administration of Franklin Delano Roosevelt she had been the president's trusted friend and adviser, and she had founded the National Council of Negro Women.

The high school Barbara attended was named for another famous black woman, Phillis Wheatley. Born in Africa, Phillis Wheatley was kidnapped at the age of eight and brought to the United States as a slave. She wrote her first poem when she was fourteen, in perfect English. A few years later she became the first black, the first slave, and the second woman ever to publish a book of poetry in America.

Reading about these people reinforced in Barbara's mind what her father had taught her. If she was willing to work hard for it, she could be almost anything, and one day during her sophomore year in high school she decided what she wanted to be.

Each year the school held a Career Day. Blacks from various professions were invited to come and speak to the students. By explaining what their careers were like, what talents or aptitudes were needed, they tried to help the students make their own career decisions. In retrospect, the very idea of a Career Day for black high school students in Texas in 1950 seems painfully overhopeful. Although opportunities were gradually beginning to open up in some fields, career choices for black youth were severely limited. Most would end up as laborers and domestic workers. Teaching was the only truly open profession. Black doctors were needed, for white doctors often refused to treat black patients. A career in the armed services was possible, but there were no black officers. More blacks were entering the legal profession, and there was a small but growing movement toward establishing equal rights for blacks in the courts. Because of this situation, the administration at Phillis Wheatley High School had invited Edith Sampson, a black lawyer from Chicago, to speak to the students.

That a busy woman would travel all the way from Chicago to speak to a group of high school students in Texas attests to her great interest in encouraging black youth, particularly young black women, to enter law. Edith Spurlock Sampson knew they needed that encouragement, and she hoped to show them that if she could succeed in the legal profession, then so could they. She had been born in Pittsburgh, Pennsylvania, and had attended school in New York and Chicago. She received her Master of Law degree from Loyola University in Chicago, the first woman of any race to receive that degree from the institution. She had begun her law practice in Chicago in 1926, specializing in criminal law and domestic relations, and had served as an assistant referee in Cook County Juvenile Court. In

1947 she had been the first black woman to be appointed an assistant state's attorney in Cook County. Just prior to speaking to the students at Phillis Wheatley High School, she was appointed by President Truman as an American alternate delegate to the United Nations. Some years later, she would become Judge Edith Sampson.

Barbara listened intently to this black woman lawyer from Chicago and scrutinized her closely. Edith Sampson was a large woman, with a pleasant face and an impressive bearing. Her voice was as compelling as her argument—if I can do it, so can you. Barbara could identify with this woman. She could imagine her own large frame attired in a neat tailored suit, imagine the sound of her own already judicious voice commanding the attention of a courtroom or auditorium audience. Edith Sampson was something special. Barbara decided she wanted to be a lawyer.

When Barbara confided her ambition to be a lawyer to her parents, she met mixed reactions. Arlyne Jordan was against the idea, for she did not think it was the right thing for a girl to do. Her two other daughters had pursued careers proper for women. They would marry and lead a secure, black middle-class existence. Law was a profession for men; she was not sure her youngest daughter could make it as a lawyer.

Hearing her mother's reaction, Barbara sighed. Like her sisters, Bennie and Rose Mary, she had taken music lessons from a private tutor for years. But though she enjoyed music, she knew a career in it just wasn't for her. She'd told her parents so.

Benjamin Jordan, on the other hand, was pleased. While he shared his wife's fears that Barbara had chosen a difficult path for herself, he had no thought of trying to keep her from it. Barbara recalls, "My father said I should do whatever I thought I could."

In June 1952 Barbara Jordan graduated from Phillis Wheatley High School in the top 5 percent of her class. She was determined to be "something outstanding," and there was no doubt in her mind that she would be.

2 College and Law School

The Jordan family had discussed the matter at length. If Barbara was going to be a lawyer, she would have to take her undergraduate degree at a school in Houston. That way she could live at home and avoid the costs of room and board, and the money saved could be put toward law school tuition. Barbara would have preferred a more prestigious school, but she understood the finances involved. There were no scholarships or fellowships available to an ambitious young black woman in those days, so Barbara went to all-black Texas Southern University in Houston and lived at home during her four years there.

In 1952 Texas Southern was a new school, although it could trace its beginnings to 1927, when Houston Colored Junior College was founded. In 1934 it became Houston College for Negroes, then Texas State University for Negroes in 1947. It had been called Texas Southern University since 1951, but it was still an all-black school whose primary purpose, in the minds of Houston whites, was to fill the need for black higher education without endangering the all-white status of the University of Texas at Houston. T.S.U. was a small school, and that was good for its students, for each could excel, if he or she wanted to, in some area of campus life.

Arriving at T.S.U., Barbara wasted no time in pursuing her goal of being "outstanding": She ran for president of the freshman class. Positive she was the best candidate, she studied the issues of interest to the students; formed her opinions on them; and in speeches urging fellow freshmen to vote for her, amazed her listeners with her talent for oratory.

Though still a teen-ager, Barbara had a commanding voice. Years of listening to her father preach had taught her how to use her voice to best advantage—how to change tone and timbre to emphasize a point. Through her reading she also had acquired an excellent vocabulary. She could say in one sentence what it took others, casting about for the right words, several sentences to say. She had already demonstrated her gift for oratory in high school, where she had won the

Julius Levy Oratorical Contest. The award would prove to be the first of many.

Andrew Jefferson, now a Houston lawyer, ran against her in the election and won. "She claims I stole that election from her to this day," he says. It is unlikely that the freshman class officers election at T.S.U. in the fall of 1952 was the scene of any political "dirty tricks." It is much more likely that Andrew Jefferson was elected president because he was a male. In that pre–women's liberation era most males *and* females believed it was proper for presidents of anything to be male. It is also likely that Andrew Jefferson won the election because he was generally better liked. Barbara Jordan was an extremely serious young woman, not given to social chitchat or campaign-style jokes. A freshman class election was, and is, essentially a popularity contest. Fellow freshmen had little doubt that Barbara Jordan was bright and articulate, but she was not as personally popular among them as was her opponent. That is not to say that Barbara had no friends. Though she kept to herself a lot and did not enjoy a wide assortment of friends, she did have a few.

Barbara did not try to get into campus politics after her freshman defeat. Instead, she concentrated on areas that demanded great individual skill and less popularity. She joined the Sigma Pi Alpha Forensic and Dialectical Symposium and the debating team. In these activities she excelled. "She was a champion debater at T.S.U.," Andrew Jefferson recalls. "We won all the prizes then, every year Barbara was on the team, and we even debated Harvard. T.S.U. has never had such a team. We've never been that good since, and Barbara tells the debate coach that all the time."

Barbara was awarded a plaque for being "the most valuable participant" in the Southern Intercollegiate Forensic Conference at Baylor University in 1954, and she was the inspiration of the T.S.U. team as it made tours to test its skill against the nation's best college debating teams, including the University of Chicago, the University of Iowa, and Harvard.

"The best we could do against Harvard was a tie," Barbara recalls. But the Harvard team must have been a bit surprised at even that outcome of a debate between its team and that of an all-black southern school, and more than a little surprised at the oratorical ability of a T.S.U. junior named Barbara Jordan.

Each year her skill at oratory increased, her command of language expanded. After a while, word got around campus: Never get into an argument with Barbara Jordan. Her campus activities indicated leadership of the responsible kind. She joined Delta Sigma Theta sorority—in the early 1950s almost everyone belonged to a sorority or fraternity—and later was named to one of the most important offices, dean of pledges. She was elected member-at-large to the Student Council, for she had no close personal ties to any segment of the student population and was thus capable of representing all of them.

Meanwhile, as a government major with a law career in mind, Barbara Jordan was becoming increasingly aware of how politics and law affected black people in America and of the possibilities for change in those areas. In 1954, midway through her undergraduate years, the Supreme Court of the United States ruled in *Brown* v. *Topeka Board of Education* that "separate but equal" educational facilities were not and could not be equal and thus were unconstitutional. In handing down such a decision, the Court struck down an earlier decision made in 1895 that had established segregation in the United States by allowing separate but supposedly equal facilities. That decision, known as *Plessy* v. *Ferguson*, had been made in a case involving public transportation in which the question was whether or not it was constitutional to assign separate streetcars for blacks. It was later applied to nearly every other public facility imaginable, from schools to theaters to drinking fountains. The 1954 *Brown* decision would have similarly widespread application. If "separate but equal" schools were unconstitutional, then so were segregated public transportation, restaurants, theaters, and so on.

As a result of the 1954 *Brown* decision Barbara Jordan did a lot of thinking. For one thing, she thought about the practice of law and the contribution black lawyers had made to the case. Thurgood Marshall, a black lawyer who would later become the first black Supreme Court justice, had been a key figure in pursuing the case, working with other lawyers of the National Association for the Advancement of Colored People. The *Brown* decision would be followed by many other cases in which equal rights for blacks would be sought. Black lawyers would be involved in these cases too, and Barbara hoped to be among them. Perhaps she would one day plead a case for equal rights before the courts.

The *Brown* decision also caused Barbara Jordan to reflect on the Constitution. Its framers had neglected to mention her and her people, but the document they had written nevertheless contained enough flexibility to allow for questions affecting the rights of her people to be decided based on its tenets. As she said in her famous "Constitution speech" in the summer of 1974, "through the process of amendment, interpretation, and court decision I have finally been included in 'We, the people.' "

A lot of hard work would go into bringing about the processes of amendment, interpretation, and court decision. The country did not simply do an about-face as a result of the *Brown* ruling. The next years would see great upheaval as blacks, and some whites, challenged the long-held customs and beliefs of black inferiority and second-class citizenship. The upheaval began in Montgomery, Alabama, late in 1955. A black woman named Rosa Parks was arrested on a Montgomery bus for refusing to give up her seat to a white man. In response, Montgomery blacks, led by a young minister named Martin Luther King, Jr., boycotted the buses, refusing to ride on them again until they were treated equally with whites. A little over a year later the Supreme Court ruled that segregation on buses was illegal, and the black people of Montgomery boarded the buses once more.

Blacks across the country had followed closely the progress of the Montgomery bus boycott. Students at T.S.U. and the people of Houston's black community were no exception. The thought crossed their minds that similar nonviolent action could be taken in their own community, but they did not ponder the notion seriously. Change can be a frightening thing, and they were well aware of the costs of the Montgomery blacks' actions. Dr. King's home had been bombed, and he and ninety-two other leaders of the boycott had been arrested and indicted. Most blacks continued to feel that accommodation to white society's policies of segregation and discrimination was still the safest and sanest course. As for Barbara herself, her chief priority was her education, and she studied long hours to make the high grades that would gain her admittance to a good law school. "I wanted to go east to school," she says, "and Harvard Law was considered the best law school in 1956." Harvard Law School was her first choice.

Harvard did not accept her. Her rejection was not necessarily because she was a woman—Harvard Law had graduated its first female students in 1950. It was not necessarily because she was black—Harvard Law had graduated blacks before. But she was a woman and black and from an all-black southern college, and those were not the best credentials for acceptance. "They [acted as if they] had never heard of Texas Southern University," she says, "and at that time it was not absolutely the fashionable thing to have black people in your student body." Boston University Law School did accept her. It was a good school and an eastern school, and she was relatively satisfied. As she had hoped, she would have a chance to experience another part of the country.

Barbara graduated from T.S.U. in June 1956 with a B.A. in government, magna cum laude. She was editor of the yearbook, which contained several photographs of her as a member of various organizations. She has changed little in appearance since that time. Tall, serious, competent-looking, she dominates her group photographs. In her senior picture she has a half smile, but her eyes are unsmiling, self-assured, and the angle of her head communicates her intention to be "something outstanding."

Barbara's education had become something of a family project. Not only her father but her two sisters as well were helping to finance her tuition and room and board at B.U., for there were still no scholarships or fellowships available to her. Neighbors and friends marveled at the Jordan family's determination, realizing how hard it was for them during those years. Barbara was also aware of the financial sacrifices her family was making, and she resolved to make them worthwhile. To excel at B.U. Law School in competition with students from the best schools in the East, she had to work harder than the others. But she was used to working hard for what she wanted.

"Things always seemed so easy for Barbara," a fellow student remembers, "at least in class or debating or at exam time." But he adds, "Those who knew her best in college knew that she was studying while we slept. There was many a night in law school when her roommate would get up in the morning and find Barbara still studying."

There was little time for social life, and club activities at law school are minimal. Except for occasional breaks for singing or playing the guitar with a few friends, Barbara did little else but eat, sleep a little, and study a lot. Three grueling years later, in 1959, she graduated from B.U. Law School with an L.L.B. degree.

After graduation Barbara taught school for a summer while she studied for the Massachusetts bar exam. She took and passed the exam in order to be licensed to practice law in that state, but Barbara really had no intention of remaining in the East. To be sure, the comparative lack of discrimination and segregation in the East appealed to her. Boston, being a college town, provided a welcoming atmosphere to black students. There were many students, and they were intent on learning, questioning. A sense of camaraderie pervaded

Barbara Jordan (center, front)
with members of the Jordan family.

the town, the students more concerned with their similarities than their differences. But Barbara realized remaining in Boston would be almost too easy. She missed her family, and while she did not like the patterns of segregation that obtained in Houston, she understood them. She could live with them while at the same time working to alter them.

"If there was nothing for me to do but practice law and make money I would have stayed in Boston," she says, "but I have to be relevant."

Barbara wanted to help people like those with whom she had grown up, and there were a lot of unfair and antiquated laws in Texas that needed changing. The groundswell for changing laws that were unfair to blacks was slowly creating the conditions under which those changes could be accomplished.

During Barbara's years at law school the civil rights movement had begun to gather momentum. Shortly after the Supreme Court decision outlawing segregation on the Montgomery, Alabama, buses, more than a hundred southerners, most of them black ministers, met in Atlanta, Georgia, to discuss the fight for equal rights. Out of this meeting came the Southern Christian Leadership Conference (S.C.L.C.), whose stated goal was "full citizenship rights and total integration of the Negro into American life." For the next few years S.C.L.C. supported bus boycotts in many southern towns and cities and joined with the older organization, the National Association for the Advancement of

Colored People, in campaigning to register millions of black voters. While she had followed the southern movement with interest, Barbara had been too busy studying to consider active involvement, and by the time she graduated from law school the N.A.A.C.P.'s legal battles for desegregation in Houston were over.

The voter registration drives, however, were not over, and they interested her. There were millions of black people old enough to vote. If they could be persuaded to register, they could gain considerable recognition from political candidates as an important voting bloc. They could make a difference in local, state, even national politics, and with their political leverage, they could help bring about changes within the system. At the end of the summer of 1959, Barbara returned home to Houston, with a Boston accent that enhanced the commanding quality of her oratory and with a determination to put her skills and energies to work at making those changes.

3 Big Hopes...

The first thing Barbara Jordan did upon returning to Houston was to study for the Texas bar exam. Because Texas had some of the strangest and most complicated laws of any state, passing the exam was not easy. Even those students who studied at Texas law schools, and thus concentrated on Texas law, found the exam hard to pass. It was not uncommon for candidates for the Texas bar to take the exam two or three times before passing it. Barbara passed the exam the first time.

Licensed now to practice law in her home state, Barbara did not have the money to open an office of her own. In fact she barely had enough money to have a stack of business cards printed with BARBARA JORDAN, ATTORNEY AT LAW. She began her practice on her parents' dining room table. It was hard to attract clients at first, but gradually friends of the family began to come to her and to recommend her, in turn, to their friends. She handled a variety of problems— real estate sales, business matters, domestic relations. In divorce cases her first interest was to explore the possibilities of reconciliation. Her favorite cases were adoptions. "The happiness that goes with adopting a baby or a child brings joy to everyone who had a part in helping to make it possible," she said.

At the same time Barbara was taking steps to establish herself within the Houston legal profession. She joined the American Bar Association and the Houston Lawyers Association, and in 1960 she got involved in politics. It was a presidential election year. Former Vice-President Richard M. Nixon was seeking the office vacated by two-term President Dwight D. Eisenhower. His Democratic opponent was John F. Kennedy. Across the country blacks were restive, aware of the gradual growth of the movement for equal rights. John Kennedy promised to support the fight for those rights. Just at the time when blacks were feeling the possibility of asserting themselves, a presidential candidate came along who seemed worth asserting themselves for. Black Texans had an additional reason for backing the Democratic slate—John Kennedy's vice-presidential running mate was Lyndon Baines Johnson, U.S. senator from Texas, a man who, despite his geographical origins, was as firmly committed to the civil rights cause as Kennedy.

Like most women in politics Barbara Jordan began her political career stuffing envelopes, running mimeograph machines, and doing all the other menial tasks traditionally regarded by male politicians as "women's work." She did her work and did not complain, waiting for an opportunity to prove her effectiveness.

That opportunity came soon. Barbara recalls: "One night we went to a church to enlist Negro voters and the woman who was supposed to speak didn't show up. I volunteered to speak in her place and right after that they took me off the stamp licking and addressing."

Late in the summer the word came down from the Democratic organization that the black vote could carry the election for Kennedy and Johnson, and it was up to black Democrats to get out that vote. Barbara was given directorship of the "Get Out the Vote" drive in Houston's black community. It was the first such drive, and she had little advice to rely on regarding how to go about it. She certainly didn't have much experience herself. But she'd always had organizational ability, and she put it to work at this time. She launched a one-person-per-block precinct drive, finding blacks who were willing to drum up votes on their own blocks and getting out lists of eligible voters and leaflets to help them in their campaign. She attacked the problem just as she had attacked her studies at school. She worked until midnight or one or two o'clock in the morning, as long as it took to get the job done. "Whatever people may believe is needed in our country, they should believe strongly enough to work for it," she says.

Kennedy and Johnson won the election by a slim margin, but they won just the same. Looking at the vote tallies from the precincts in which she had conducted her voting drive, Barbara felt pride that she had been instrumental in the Democratic victory. Just as important, she had proved her abilities to the Harris County Democratic Party organization.

Within the next year and a half, Barbara's position and influence in Houston grew. By 1962 she had strengthened her law practice and accumulated enough money to open her own office at 4100 Lyons Avenue, not far from her home. A second-floor walk-up above a print shop, whose sign read KNOCK & HOLLER, her office was nevertheless her own. It was shabby at first, but over the years she would install pine paneling, a red carpet, and air conditioning. Among her first additions to the decor were framed color photographs of John F. Kennedy and Lyndon B. Johnson. They would remain on her walls long after both men were no longer in the White House.

By early 1962 Barbara had been elected president of the all-black Houston Lawyers Association, despite the fact that she was the sole woman member and only twenty-six years old. The reasoning behind her election by her fellow members was simple: "Get Barbara to do it, and you know it'll be done right," as one of the association's leaders said. Similar respect for her abilities led to her appointment as second vice-chairman of the Harris County Democrats and a board member of the Houston Council on Human Relations.

Armed with these credentials and a self-assurance remarkable for the average twenty-six-year-old but expected in Barbara Jordan, she announced her candidacy for the Democratic nomination for state representative, Position 10, on February 3, 1962. That no other black woman before her had ever campaigned for the nomination did not daunt her. That no other black had served in the Texas House since Reconstruction concerned her even less. She was bright, she was a hard worker, she had a clear platform, and she felt she would do a better job than those against whom she was running in the May 5th Democratic primary: a former assistant district attorney named Willis Whatley—her major opponent—and a Church of Christ minister, Jim Shock. She was so confident that she even, in a sense, ran against her own party: She announced she was running as an independent Democrat "who feels strong enough to resist pressures which most certainly will be brought to bear on candidates supported by the slate."

She had almost no money. In fact she had borrowed the $500 filing fee to become a candidate for the seat. The drawing of the county political lines was also against her. Unlike counties in many other states, counties in Texas were not divided into districts. Even in a populous area like Harris County, which included Houston, representatives were elected county-wide, which meant that all of the over one million eligible voters voted for each representative. Under this system, some parts of the country had no local representatives, while other parts had too many. Political experts gave her no chance of winning, but still Barbara Jordan was confident: "In my political naïveté I believed that I was more articulate than my opponent and sensitive to people's needs and aspirations. These qualities, I felt, would help me overcome the odds against my election to the Texas House."

During the next three months Barbara campaigned for the Democratic nomination, speaking before women's groups, Y.W.C.A. meetings, United Fund agencies, anywhere that she could be heard; and everywhere she was heard, she moved her audience with her commanding presence and her no-nonsense presentation of the issues.

But she was not really prepared for the personal questions she received. Suddenly her family, her school career, her personal likes and dislikes, were of interest. Barbara did not like such prying. She would give her qualifications readily, but her private life was another matter. She would speak at length only about the books she had read:

"I found that *A Shade of Difference* by Alan Drury had so much of an aura of reality that it became fascinating reading. *Failsafe,* another best seller, is similarly an enjoyable, if disturbing, story.

"I'd also like to mention *Nobody Knows My Name,* the collection of essays by James Baldwin. This expression of raw and naked tenderness by a Negro sort of laid my soul bare. I could see this man struggling with himself, and I could feel with him in what he was trying to do."

Barbara Jordan based her campaign on issues. The most important one, in her eyes, was that of welfare reform:

> It's so unfair to see the really handicapped people starving while so many others—who are able to make their own way—are getting a free ride on the state's welfare rolls. There are thousands of persons in this state who just can't feed and clothe themselves because of old age or physical handicap. I'll do everything I can in the legislature to see that these people are taken care of. At the same time I'll see what can be done about striking from our welfare rolls the people who are just trying to get out of work. If this group were stricken from the rolls, the ones who go hungry and hopeless could be taken care of.

Other aims in her campaign included abolition of the poll tax, which she felt discriminated against eligible but poor voters; an increase in the state's minimum-wage law; revision of the sales tax law; and equal

property rights for women. She addressed herself to no
particular group, and indeed, felt no allegiance to any
particular group. Her allegiance was to her vision of a
better Texas:

> My hope as a member of the legislature is to have
> a part in making Texas a better state for all of
> her ten million people. We have the oil, the land,
> the trees, the manpower, the brains, the good will,
> to improve the level of living for all. We can
> make better use of what we have—not by taking
> anything away from anyone, but by creating more,
> so that the share of each is greater.

In her commanding voice she stated these aims over
and over, but she never had an opportunity to debate
Whatley. "I rarely saw my opponent in person," she
recalls, "but I was confronted by his face on many
billboards and on the television screen. He was obviously well financed."

Considerable money was needed for a county-wide
campaign. To reach all the people, a candidate needed
billboards and television coverage. Even with a dedi-
cated volunteer organization Barbara could not hope
to reach through speeches and leaflets and doorbell
ringing as many people as could her opponent. She
recalls, with the air of someone who has learned an
important political lesson: "I felt that if politicians
were believable and pressed the flesh [shook hands]
to the maximum extent possible, the people would over-

look race, sex, and poverty—and elect me. They did not."

Barbara received 46,000 votes; Willis Whatley got 65,000. She tried to rationalize her defeat: "I figured anybody who could get 46,000 people to vote for them for any office should keep on trying," she said ten years later. But back in 1962 her rationalizations had a hollow ring, even to her own ears.

There was some consolation. While she was unable to take the active political role she desired, and while she resented the conditions that prevented blacks in general from participating equally in the political process, she was nevertheless pleased with the national administration. John F. Kennedy had said, in speaking of social and racial conditions in the United States, "We can do more," and he was providing examples of that belief, encouraging Martin Luther King, Jr., in his fight for equal rights for blacks, inaugurating programs to help poor people of all races, and introducing into Congress bills to benefit minorities and the poor. One of his most "visible" acts had been to support black Congressman Adam Clayton Powell, ranking majority member of the House Education and Labor Committee, for the chairmanship of that committee, against considerable opposition even from members of his and Powell's Democratic Party. During the 1962 campaign Barbara had publicly supported Kennedy-type programs in Texas. In November 1963 the president was scheduled to visit Texas, and she was pleased about the recognition he would bring to the cause of black and poor people in the state.

On November 22, 1963, John F. Kennedy was killed by an assassin's bullet as he rode with Texas Governor John Connally in an open car through the streets of Dallas. The tragedy stunned the country. The young president had inspired many people and given them the sort of hope and belief in their country that they had not had before. Especially bitter for Texans, particularly blacks, was the fact that John Kennedy had been killed in their state.

Vice-President Lyndon Johnson took the oath of office as president on Air Force One, en route from Dallas to Washington, while the body of the slain president rested in the rear. Johnson was well-liked among Texas blacks, and they were disturbed that he would assume the presidency under the shadow of his predecessor's death. Later, once the initial period of grief was over, there was speculation about what Johnson would do as president. Would he continue the programs and changes begun under Kennedy? All anyone could do was wait and see.

Meanwhile Barbara continued her law practice, maintained her active roles in the Houston Lawyers Association and the Harris County Democratic organization, and increased her schedule of speaking engagements. She intended to run for the Texas House again in 1964, and saw the advantages in starting early, in gaining through time and hard work what well-financed

*Lyndon Johnson takes the oath of office
aboard Air Force One following
the assassination of John F. Kennedy.*

campaigns could attain for their candidates through billboard and television advertising.

On January 25, 1964, she once again announced her candidacy for the Texas legislature, Position 10, the position held by Willis Whatley, who had defeated her two years before.

"It is urgent that the legislature become more responsive to the needs of the people of Texas," she said in her announcement speech. "Skilled lobbyists speak for every kind of interest except that of the average citizen. The real need is to make it possible for all Texans to become more productive. Education, job training, and the elimination of the burden of discrimination will help."

The specific issues in her platform were the same as they had been in 1962. Why? Because nothing had been done about them in the two years since she had last run.

This time Barbara was a more experienced candidate. She had built up a large volunteer organization and she held open houses at her campaign headquarters to attract more workers. She realized that as a black female candidate she was not even taken seriously by many voters, and certainly not by the political "establishment," but she thought that this time she could persuade some of the purveyors of public opinion to remain neutral.

"I went to the newspaper publishers and acknowledged their probable difficulty in supporting me editorially but urged them not to support my opponent—just to take a chance on the people making the best choice," Barbara recalls. "One of the major papers in Houston made no endorsement; the other endorsed my opponent."

In the election Barbara received 66,000 votes, but Willis Whatley still received more. She had lost again. Her supporters reminded her that the decision of one major Houston newspaper to remain neutral was something of a victory. They also pointed out that a respectable percentage of the 20,000 more votes she had received this time had come from traditionally white, conservative areas. But that did not make Barbara feel much better about her two losses in a row.

Up in New York Shirley Chisholm had won election to the State Assembly, the second black woman to be elected to that body. Elsewhere in the North and the East, blacks were beginning to win elective offices on local and state levels. The movement would reach the South and West eventually, Barbara's supporters assured her. That didn't make her feel any better either. She was, as she remembers, "dispirited."

"I considered abandoning the dream of a political career in Texas and moving to some section of the country where a black woman candidate was less likely to be considered a novelty. I didn't *want* to do this. I am a Texan; my roots are in Texas. To leave would be a cop-out."

4...Realized

Barbara stayed in Texas. She resumed her law practice, but it remained small and not particularly lucrative. When she was offered a job as an administrative assistant to Harris County Judge Bill Elliott, she eagerly accepted it, becoming the first black to be appointed to such a high county position. And it was a position with real responsibilities, "not," as Barbara once put it, "as head Negro in charge of nothing."

As administrative assistant for welfare, her job was to coordinate the activities of the various welfare agencies and projects in Harris County. It involved luncheons, meetings, talking with people in need of welfare, and was very different from her law practice, in which she had dealt mainly with individuals and with the courts.

"I'm enjoying it," she said after a month on the job, "and I have no regrets about leaving law practice. In this job I feel I can help more people reach meaningful solutions to welfare problems."

She had other reasons for accepting the job. Her father had retired, and aware of the sacrifices he had made to finance her schooling, she was eager to help him now that he was no longer working. Most of all, however, she wanted to prove to him that his sacrifices had been worthwhile, that she would indeed become something outstanding. At times she despaired that she ever could.

Conditions had improved for blacks and women, but there were still many barriers before them. Had Barbara tried to run for the Texas legislature ten years earlier, she probably would have been laughed out of Houston. In 1962 and 1964 her prospects were greater, but the barriers presented by the Texas county electoral system counteracted the growing willingness of Texas voters to put aside considerations of race and sex in selecting their representatives. There were still many inequities under which blacks in Texas had to live.

Most Houston whites did not recognize those inequities, or if they did, they did not consider them improper. On the whole, white Houston was proud of its progress in desegregation of public facilities, restaurants, theaters, and hotels. The municipal golf course had been desegregated in 1950; the public library had integrated its facilities in 1953; segregation on city buses had ended in 1954; discrimination in city-owned buildings was eliminated in 1962. There hadn't been a protest demonstration since 1960; and though desegregation of the schools was proceeding slowly, the black wards in the city, with a greater population than in any other city in the South, seemed quiet. At a March 1965 conference of mayors Houston Mayor Louie Welch stated confidently, "We have no race problem in Houston."

Mayor Welch was in for a surprise. Less than two months later, on May 10, more than 9,000 students stayed away from their black high schools and hundreds of blacks marched through the city to protest school segregation. As they marched, they sang the freedom songs that had become familiar in the rest of the South but had never before been heard in Houston.

Houston's officials, and its white population in general, could not understand the protest. They had thought they knew what was going on in the black communities. They hadn't realized they only knew what a small group of black leaders *told* them was going on.

These acknowledged black leaders numbered no more than half a dozen. The oldest was in his eighties, the youngest in his fifties. For years they had been the primary channel through which Houston blacks had communicated with Houston's white leaders. They had voiced Negroes' complaints about unpaved streets and poor city services, police brutality, lack of representation in government and business, and had, as the Houston *Chronicle* put it, "been invited behind closed doors to receive, on behalf of the Negro community, desegregation of public places, theaters, restaurants, hotels."

In the days when ordinary black people had no voice, these leaders served a valuable function. Their diplomatic, accommodating style was the only way to approach the white leadership, and if it had not been for them there would have been little or no communication between the races. These men, businessmen and ministers, had occupied a special position, aloof from the general black population. For many years blacks had believed that was the way leaders should be. But the civil rights movement and Negro gains in the early 1960s—gains that had been accomplished frequently by activity on the grass-roots level—had brought about a change in most blacks' opinions regarding the characteristics of good leaders. By 1964, many Houston blacks believed their leaders should be aggressive rather than accommodating, people with whom they could identify rather than people who were aloof. They began to look to a new, younger leadership, leaders who could help them build quickly on the gains they had made. As Barbara once said, "Change we must, the young people are on our heels. They are saying to us, 'We don't want any more of your old-fashioned shucking and jiving and we aren't having any more of the old-fashioned acceptable Negroes.' " Barbara Jordan was of the new type of leadership.

The idea of boycotting the schools was that of thirty-six-year-old Reverend William Lawson, and he had begun his campaign by meeting with fewer than fifty students at a single school. As the campaign had gained momentum, he had contacted others to help him. Barbara had known him at T.S.U., where he had arrived in 1955 as a student rector. In the boycott she served on his strategy committee, and in the march that represented the culmination of the boycott campaign she strode purposively with him at the head and sang freedom songs in her commanding voice.

When he learned of the march, Mayor Welch hurried to the school administration building to wait for the protestors. They marched right past him. One of the older black community leaders had joined the front lines of the marchers, and as they neared the school district offices, he offered to act as a liaison between Reverend Lawson and Mayor Welch. Lawson ignored him completely. "It was at that moment," said one observer, "that Lawson took the leadership [of the black community]."

Desegregation of Houston's public schools proceeded more rapidly after that, the schools completing desegregation in 1966–1967, and for the black community as a whole there was a feeling of greater control over their own lives. While Barbara Jordan was pleased about the progress, she was still concerned about the political situation of blacks in Houston and about the progress of her own political career.

Between 1964 and 1966 changes in national laws and the enforcement in Texas of civil rights laws passed earlier altered the state's electoral system and removed the barriers that had prevented Barbara Jordan from realizing her goals. The civil rights movement had steadily gained momentum since 1959, when a group of students chiefly from black southern colleges had formed the Student Nonviolent Coordinating Committee (S.N.C.C.) and started massive voter registration drives in Mississippi, Georgia, and Alabama. Resistance on the part of whites in these states was frightening in its ferocity. Young workers, black and white, as well as the blacks whom they were trying to register, were taunted by police, threatened by white citizens' groups, arrested, jailed, beaten. Some were even killed. In Mississippi during the summer of 1964, S.N.C.C. and its supporters suffered at least one thousand arrests, thirty-five shootings, eight beatings, and six murders. But the students kept on working and the eligible black voters kept on registering, and after a while the violence in the South caused revulsion in the rest of the country. "It is wrong—deadly wrong—to deny any of your fellow Americans the vote," said President Lyndon Johnson. A few months later he signed the Voting

Rights Act of 1965. It eliminated the poll tax and pledged the support of federal troops in registering all those eligible voters who wished to register.

Texas had not experienced the strident racial confrontations that had occurred in other parts of the South. Nevertheless, many of its eligible black voters had been unable to afford the poll tax, and many others had been apathetic about voting. Now, convinced that at least the federal government wanted a black voice in electoral politics, they were eager to register to vote, an eagerness that was highly encouraging to black aspirants to political office in Texas.

Even more encouraging was the reapportionment of state House and Senate districts that occurred in Texas. In March 1962 the Supreme Court had ruled in a case known as *Baker* v. *Carr* that counties in the southern states should be divided into districts according to population so as to make the ideal system of one man—one vote a reality. Although the decision did not cover Texas, a southwestern state, and the Texas system of dividing the state only by county lines, representing acreage rather than people, continued for a time, *Baker* stimulated more black voter registration in Texas, too, and made a change in its system inevitable. In 1965 the system called for under the *Baker* ruling was introduced to Texas and the state was reapportioned. Suddenly Barbara Jordan found herself living in a newly created state senatorial district, the 11th. It was 38 percent black, with the rest of the population

Chicano and white, and it contained 70 percent of the precincts that she had carried in the 1962 and 1964 elections. No doubt about it, Barbara Jordan would run for a seat in the Texas Senate.

Naturally she was not the only one who wanted the new Senate seat. The creation of a new seat or office always results in a scramble for it. State Representative J. C. Whitfield also announced his intention to run. "He called me before the filing deadline and asked if I was planning to run for the Senate," Barbara remembers. "I said I was. He said he was going to run no matter what I did. It was a friendly and candid conversation." Whitfield formally filed as a candidate on December 20.

Barbara did not file for another month and a half. There were matters to be attended to first, such as changing jobs. She had been offered a position with the Crescent Foundation, a private, nonprofit corporation under contract with the Department of Labor. A grant of $360,000 had been made to the foundation for a special project to aid "hard-core unemployables," and the foundation needed people to direct and coordinate the project. Barbara was hired as project coordinator at a salary of $10,000 per year. The project director would be Otis H. King, who had been a classmate of Barbara's at T.S.U. Back at Texas Southern University, Barbara and King had been together on the varsity debating team; now, some ten years later, they were together again.

Barbara resigned her position as administrative assistant to County Judge Bill Elliott at the end of December and at just about the same time announced her intention to run for the 11th District Senate seat. "Having received the overwhelming support of this same district when I campaigned for a seat in the legislature two years and four years ago," she said, "gives me confidence that this time those who have supported me will succeed." Still, she waited to file formally as a candidate. First she wanted to make sure it was legal and proper for her to work at the foundation and run for the Senate at the same time. She did not feel J. C. Whitfield would get much of a head start campaigning. Based on their telephone conversation she anticipated a tough but clean fight with him. It would prove to be otherwise.

On February 4, 1966, Barbara paid her $1,000 filing fee as a candidate for the Texas Senate in the Democratic primary contest. For the press it was a little-noticed act, but Barbara Jordan realized it was a historic occasion. Not since Reconstruction had a Negro been a candidate for the Senate. She had asked Lonnie E. Smith to be with her as she filed. Smith, a Houston dentist, had been the plaintiff in the case of *Smith* v. *Allwright*, the 1944 decision which had given blacks the right to vote in the Democratic primary in Texas.

Barbara's 1966 campaign for public office was considerably different from her two previous campaigns.

For one thing the Texas Senate was far more exclusive and influential than the Texas House. Indeed, it was considered the state's most exclusive club. For another her opponent for the Democratic nomination this time was a liberal. Unlike her opponent in the two previous elections, J. C. Whitfield believed in many of the same causes in which she believed and had demonstrated his stand on the issues as a state representative.

But soon Whitfield and a group of other liberal Democrats proved that in reality they were not quite as "liberal" as they had previously represented themselves as being. The reapportionment of Harris County had changed the lines of power within the Harris County Democratic Committee. When the committee met in March to decide which of the Democratic primary candidates they would endorse, Whitfield and some other candidates for the legislature asked for co-endorsement of nine candidates, which meant that the committee would endorse both Whitfield *and* Barbara Jordan for the same seat.

Many on the committee opposed the idea. They wanted to endorse the slate supported by a Democratic coalition composed of representatives of labor groups, Latin American groups, and the Harris County Council of Negro Organizations, a slate that included the name of Barbara Jordan. In reaction to their opposition an angry Whitfield changed his stance and claimed Barbara Jordan had no qualifications for endorsement and did not truly represent the people.

With that Barbara rose. In her commanding voice and appearing to look every member of the gathering straight in the eye, she said: "I live in this district and I was born in this district and these are the people I am representative of." The crowd rose to give her a standing ovation, one of four she received that night.

Angered by their inability to influence the meeting, Whitfield and about fifty others walked out and announced the establishment of a rival liberal Democratic organization, the East Side Democrats. The split could have proved a serious one for Harris County's Democrats, particularly its liberal Democrats. Whitfield was powerful; if Barbara lost to him in the primary it was feared that many of her supporters, especially blacks, would stay away from the polls in the general election, or even possibly vote Republican in some races.

Whitfield was determined to prove that Barbara was not qualified to hold the Senate seat. Soon after the explosive Harris County Democratic Committee meeting he publicly accused her of conflict of interest. He charged that her running for the Senate seat while working as an administrator of federal funds under the War on Poverty program was improper. In telegrams to the U.S. attorney general and the secretary of labor, a copy of which he sent to the major Houston newspapers, he said: "I, as a citizen and as her opponent, request immediate investigation by your office into possible violation of federal statutes and the propriety and potential political implication of a candidate for public office having hundreds of thousands of dollars of federal funds available in her district during an election now in progress."

Barbara immediately called a press conference to answer the charges. She told the assembled reporters: "Before I took the position, I asked if there would be any conflict of interest or any reason why I should not do the work while a candidate. This was checked here and in Washington, and I was assured there was no conflict or anything wrong as long as I put in a full day's work—as I have been doing. I was the first one to raise the conflict of interest issue and was assured there was none."

Federal funds with which she was involved were all earmarked for employers to train unemployable people, she said. "I have absolutely nothing to say about disbursement of any of the funds. None of them is at my disposal."

After Barbara's response the matter was dropped. But then Whitfield tried a new tack. Bringing to public attention the ethnic makeup of the new senatorial district, he used as his slogan, "Can a white man still win?"

Barbara had always been an issue-oriented candidate and did not care to become involved in questions of personality or race or sex. But Whitfield had introduced the racial issue into the campaign and she would not let it go unanswered. Her response to his slogan

was a slogan of her own: "No, not this time." Otherwise, she refused to exploit the racial difference
between herself and her opponent. She won the Democratic primary by a vote margin of two to one (19,317
to 9,772), and though the November 8th general election was still ahead, in Texas in those days winning the
Democratic primary was tantamount to winning the
election.

On the evening of primary day, as the vote counts
came in and Barbara's victory became apparent, hundreds of friends and relatives crowded into her headquarters at the True Level Lodge on Lyons Street, and
those who could not fit inside cheered and sang in the
streets outside. Between hugs from her parents and
sisters she beamed with pleasure: "This is really great.
It's good to be a winner after two defeats for the state
House."

Among the well-wishers was County Judge Bill
Elliott. Barbara had quit her job in his office the previous December to begin her campaign, but she had
left no hard feelings behind her. "This is just a first
step for her," Elliott said on election night. "We will
be hearing a lot more from Barbara Jordan. In the
Senate she will be a credit to the Negro race, the white
race, and all the races. We're extremely happy to see
her win."

It is no longer acceptable to refer to a minority
person as "a credit to his or her race." After all, as
black people pointed out in the late 1960s, the phrase

*Barbara Jordan beams
after winning her first election.*

seems to indicate that the majority of the race are not "credits." No white person was ever described that way. Barbara was not particularly pleased with this "faint praise" in 1966, but she understood that it was well-meant. She also realized that she would be watched closely to see how she would perform in the Texas Senate. She determined not to make any mistakes.

Part of her "dignified senator" image was not to show her joy at winning. After the initial flush of victory she made only one more public statement that indicated how much of herself she had invested in the campaign. She had expected to win, she said, "but I would not allow myself to believe it, for fear I would not work as hard. I worked hard for this."

Congratulatory telephone calls and telegrams came in from the Speaker of the Texas House and ten state senators, and Lieutenant Governor Preston Smith assured her he was looking forward to working with her. "The state leadership has recognized the historical inevitability of a Negro being elected," Barbara told reporters. "They were psychologically prepared."

Although she had not as yet actually won the Senate seat, she had no Republican opponent and she hardly needed to campaign against the Constitution Party nominee, Bob Chapman. From the primary onward Barbara spoke as a newly elected state senator.

She was constantly asked how, as the only black in the Senate, she would act. "Of course I can't ignore the fact of my race—it's too evident," she would say with a smile. "Naturally I will be interested in any legislation affecting Negroes." But she intended to stand on her campaign promises to help better the lives of all Texans, particularly those who had never before had anyone to speak for them in the state legislature.

Meanwhile in other parts of the South the civil rights movement had taken a more militant turn. The Student Nonviolent Coordinating Committee had undergone an ideological split in its ranks and had changed its name to the Student *National* Coordinating Committee. In June S.N.C.C. leader Stokely Carmichael had raised a clenched fist and called for "Black Power!" a cry that had reverberated across the nation. Young blacks were tired of being beaten and arrested and not reacting, as was the nonviolent way. They had suffered much in the name of integration, and many were so sickened by white violence that they no longer wanted integration. There would soon be open talk of separatism. As part of this change many were against working "within the system," as Barbara Jordan would be doing. But for Barbara there was no conflict. "All blacks are militants in their guts," she says, "but militancy is expressed in different ways."

5 Freshman in the Texas Senate

On Tuesday, January 10, 1967, the capital city of Texas, Austin, found itself inundated with people. Swearing-in day at the state legislature had always brought relatives and well-wishers, but never anything like the crowds that converged on the city on this historic day for black Texans. For the first time since Reconstruction three black legislators would sit in the Capitol. They were Representatives Curtis Graves of Houston and Joseph Lockridge of Dallas and Senator Barbara Jordan.

Hundreds of blacks came to Austin to wish their new representatives well. They arrived in chartered buses and in private cars, some having gotten up at 4 A.M. to make the trip. Some 450 people came from Houston alone. Their two fellow Houstonites were to be sworn in, and one of them would be the first black in the Texas Senate since 1883.

Student council members from E. O. Smith Junior High School, which Barbara had attended, waited to greet her as she walked into the Capitol. The Metropolitan Senior Citizens Club of Houston sent a delegation. Perhaps these old black people could appreciate the event the most, because for the greater part of their lives there had been little hope that it could ever happen. "It's the greatest experience of my life," said one elderly man. "I stuck my chest out. I'll never forget this day. You don't know how hard I've worked for this."

Passing between lines of smiling black faces, Barbara, wearing a white orchid for the occasion, made her way into the Senate chamber. The gallery was filled with supporters. She looked for and found her mother and father, her sisters, an aunt, an uncle. She recognized other faces, but there were many she did not recognize—ordinary black people to whom her victory meant practically as much as it did to her. As she entered the chamber, they broke into cheers. "They didn't know about the rules [against demonstrations]," Barbara later explained. "I looked up at them and covered my lips with my index finger. They became quiet instantly, but continued to communicate their support by simply smiling. Finally I had won the right to represent a portion of the people in Texas."

After she had repeated the oath of office in her deep, clear voice, she was welcomed by many colleagues, who hastened over to shake her hand. All white, all male, they provided a starkly contrasting background for the newcomer. "You didn't have any trouble picking me out down there, did you?" she jokingly asked her uncle later. But as rules and meetings were discussed, she immediately became a part of the assemblage, listening intently to the points raised, although she did not say anything herself.

"I expected the first day to be devoted to routine matters," she said later. "But apparently we are off to a really fast start. I am pleased we got some issues of substance up for debate the first day." One important activity that she wished had been saved for another day was the drawing that would determine which senators would serve four-year and which would serve two-year terms. Under the Texas constitution, one half the members were elected every two years. When redistricting occurred as it had in 1965, it was necessary to hold a drawing to determine who would be the unfortunate ones.

Thirty-one numbered slips of paper were placed in a hopper. Some numbers meant four years, others two. During the drawing there was an air of nervous hilarity in the Senate chamber. Cries of "Post time!" and "Hey, what are the odds?" sounded as each senator approached the hopper and drew a slip of paper. As the number on the slip was read, the assemblage would either explode into cheers or murmur expressions of sympathy.

When Barbara's turn came, the others were quiet. She was not part of the back-slapping, "good ole boy" relationship the others enjoyed. Calmly, aware that all eyes were on her, she reached in and selected her slip. The number represented a two-year term. Her colleagues remained silent, but the sense of irony that the only black senator was one of the unlucky ones must have been running through all their minds. Barbara showed no reaction. This meant, of course, that she would have to run for office again the next year. It would be costly and time-consuming. But she decided not to worry about it until the time came.

The day's session over, she was accompanied by her supporters to her fourth-floor office in the Capitol building. Sitting in the chair behind her desk for the first time was the occasion for a ceremony, as was her every act on that very special day. She signed her autograph hundreds of times, posed for countless pictures. She was tired, but she understood how important this day was to her well-wishers, and so she serenely signed her name and endured the popping flashbulbs and smiled at the jubilation around her, and she would be just as patient during the weeks of receptions and parties that would follow. But she looked forward to the time when she would sit in session with the other senators and get down to business, when she could begin working for the changes she intended to bring about, when she could really start being a legislator.

It promised to be an interesting session. By its very smallness, the thirty-one-member Senate concentrated a great deal of power in the hands of a few. A determined group of only eleven could successfully block action on any bill, and as a result of the November election there were twelve senators generally regarded as conservative, twelve generally seen as liberal, and seven that could be described as moderates.

Each state legislature sets its own procedure and rules. In some legislatures such rules and procedures are fairly standard and relatively easy to understand. Not so in Texas. The rules of its legislature are among the most arcane and complicated in the country. They had been established by the Constitution of 1876 and had changed little since then, although twentieth-century politics was far different from that of the nineteenth century. For example, the framers of the Texas Constitution had provided for a semiannual legislature, two sessions being enough for the state lawmakers to complete their business in the 1870s. By the 1960s, however, two sessions per year just did not allow enough time for consideration of all the bills that came before each house. During the last days of each session there was a mad scramble to complete all unfinished business before the closing. Hundreds of bills were still waiting to be considered and voted on, making it necessary for the legislators to sit in session until the early morning hours and to vote on bills without having an adequate opportunity to study them.

The Texas legislature also gives its joint "conference committees" an inordinate amount of power. In most legislatures such conference committees, comprised of members of both houses, meet to work out compromises when both houses have passed very similar bills. The U.S. Congress has them. Unlike those in the U.S. Congress, however, Texas legislative conference committees are not restricted to resolving differences between similar bills. In Texas a conference committee can change every provision of both bills, and if the result is radically different from either of the original bills, it still stands and is not even subject to debate.

Some of the rules are obscure and rarely employed. Yet to the aware legislator they can come in very handy. One of the rules of the Texas House provided that five members could remove any bill from the calendar by presenting to the Speaker a written objection carrying their signatures. According to the rules of the Senate any candidate for an appointive office whose appointment had to be approved by that body could be automatically and unilaterally turned down by the senator from his or her home district.

All the rules and procedures could not be learned in a day, or even a week. One of the first things Barbara did was to study them. Every night she pored over the legislative handbooks governing rules of parliamentary procedure. Every day the legislature was in session she sat in the Senate and observed how the rules were put into practice and, generally, how more seasoned senators operated.

One of the most striking characteristics of the Texas legislature was its commitment to the interests of big business in the state. Political expert Neal Peirce once wrote, "In no other state has the control [of a single moneyed establishment] been so direct, so unambiguous, so commonly accepted." Pick any bill under consideration in the Texas legislature and chances are it was a bill that would benefit big business, whether oil, or construction, or insurance, or computers. Traditionally the money men were conservative, and they exerted their control through conservative Democrats. Though in the past decade or so, more moderate and liberal Democrats had been elected to the legislature and more progressive legislation had been passed, none of it had really hurt the money establishment. Texas was one of the few states that still had no income tax, a situation that greatly benefited the rich.

Another striking characteristic of the Texas legislature in general was its tradition of political trading off and cooperation. It was an ancient practice of the legislature that one house was obligated to approve the actions of the other unless there was some vital reason to object, and among the members of each house a similar tradition operated. The Texas House of Representatives had what was called a "pledge card system" whereby a candidate for Speaker solicited signed promises of support from his fellow members. In return he gave verbal promises of support to them. If he gained the Speakership, those whose signed promises he held were obligated to support him, sometimes for the duration of his term and sometimes against their own better judgment. Although the Texas Senate had no such formal system, the senators engaged in similar political trading off. They traded support for a fellow senator's favorite bill in exchange for that senator's vote on one of their favorite measures. Most politicians engage in this sort of dealing to some degree, but few do so with such fervor and such regularity as Texas legislators.

All of this dealing was carried on in an atmosphere of energetic, even boisterous camaraderie. There was lots of hugging and kissing and mutual praising, back slapping and joke making. The majority of the members of the Texas Senate were "good ole boys," outwardly polite, even flattering, but inwardly tough as hardtack, full of speeches about what they wanted to do for their constituencies but firmly believing their ultimate responsibility was to the money interests and to ensuring their own re-election. They were "men's men," preferring the company of men, enjoying women but expecting them to remain in their place. They socialized a great deal while the legislature was in session and welcomed the favors of the lobbyists who stalked the Capitol's halls looking for votes on measures of particular interest to the individuals and companies for whom they worked.

Barbara was certainly no stranger to the Texas "good ole boy" characteristics, and she observed their operation in the Senate. But she did not imitate them. She knew she could not be accepted as "one of the boys," and she wasn't even going to try. The only way she was going to be an effective legislator was to be one who had done her homework. Within a month senators were seeking her out to discuss parliamentary points and to get advice.

On March 15, two months after she took her oath of office, Barbara Jordan made her "maiden speech" on the floor of the Senate. Previously, she had sponsored or co-sponsored several bills—she was co-sponsor of a bill that would make it a felony to disturb people who were peacefully and lawfully picketing and sponsor of three bills affecting auto insurance for Texans—but introducing a bill does not require making a speech.

The matter of a city sales tax was before the Senate. It would allow cities to vote on whether or not they wished a one-cent city sales tax levied on their respective cities. A number of city mayors were in favor of the tax, as were a number of senators. But many senators were against the bill. Barbara was one of them. Rumor had it that these senators, all liberal Democrats, intended a filibuster on the bill, which meant that they would speak for days if necessary in order to stall action and hopefully wear down their opposition.

"Senator Jordan told me she wanted to be heard on the bill," Lieutenant Governor Preston Smith told reporters. "This is her first request to be heard. She indicated she might make some remarks."

Would she be a part of a filibuster? To the reporters' questions she answered that she was not planning a filibuster, but, then, there were others who intended to speak against the bill, too. "I have no idea how long these people will take to state their objections," she said. "I'm not planning to filibuster. I'm just planning to state all of my objections to that bill."

In her speech she called the bill "the absolute worst form of city sales tax that has been proposed in any state" and stated that it would be too great a burden on underprivileged blacks and Latin Americans, citing statistics in support of her statement.

"Forty percent of the people of this state make under $3,000 a year, which the federal government has designated as the poverty level. . . . Where is the equity in a situation where the people who earn the most pay the least tax and those who earn the least pay the most?"

It was a good speech, and delivered in Barbara's weighty, skillful manner, it was even better. Senator A. R. Schwartz praised the speech as the finest maiden speech ever made by a Texas senator in his memory. Barbara realized he might be prejudiced—he was the most vocal opponent of the bill. Still, she was pleased about his praise and quite satisfied with her speech herself. The city tax bill was passed, but not without a good fight from, among others, freshman Senator Barbara Jordan.

By now she felt comfortable as a senator. She was earning the respect of her colleagues, and that was what she wanted. She had encountered no discriminatory remarks or situations. When she was not back in Houston, she lived in a four-unit apartment building near the Capitol in which she was the only black tenant. The fact that she was black was too evident not to be noticed, but more and more she was seen as a legislator rather than as a black. She encouraged that view by not seeking out the company of her two fellow black legislators. She did not deliberately avoid them. They were in the House of Representatives, she was in the Senate. Had she sought them out, she would not have improved her legislative position and she might have opened herself to criticism for either trying to start a black "bloc," small as it was, or for being too insecure to go it alone.

Power and influence obviously did not lie in playing "black politics"—not in the Texas legislature in the late 1960s, and particularly not in the Senate. "The Texas Senate was touted as the state's most exclusive club," she recalls. "To be effective, I had to get inside the club, not just inside the chamber. I singled out the most influential and powerful members and was determined to gain their respect."

One such senator was Dorsey Hardeman of San Angelo, chairman of the Senate State Affairs Council.

"Senator Hardeman knew the rules of the Senate better than any other member," says Barbara. "In order to gain his respect, I too had to know the rules. I learned the rules."

In late April an air pollution bill was introduced in the Senate by Cris Cole of Harris County. On its face it was a good bill, intended to strengthen state and local control of air pollution. But an amendment to the bill had been introduced that would prevent anyone in Texas who was not an individual citizen or private corporation from suing either to lessen pollution or to recover damages caused by it. Cole was in favor of it. Barbara and some other senators were concerned especially that the right to sue would be denied to cities.

Barbara introduced an amendment specifying that nothing in the bill should prevent cities from having the right to sue. She admits that in seeking passage she tried to get around some of the parliamentary fine points—"a tactic," she recalls, "for which Hardeman was noted and which he practiced masterfully. I almost succeeded until Senator Hardeman started to listen to what I was saying."

"What are you trying to do?" Hardeman demanded.

Barbara looked over at the senator. "It's simple," she said. "I'm using the tricker's tricks."

Hardeman was stunned for a moment. Then he chuckled; soon he was laughing out loud. "His respect for me was affirmed at that time," says Barbara.

Cris Cole wasn't laughing. He was already angry

Texas State Senator Barbara Jordan

about the response to the amendment he favored. When he heard the text of Barbara's amendment, he became furious.

"What have the cities done with their power? Not a thing!" he shouted.

"I have more faith in the government of the city of Houston and the county of Harris than does the senator from—what is your district, Senator?" she asked of her fellow Harris County Democrat.

When used appropriately, sarcasm can be a most effective weapon. Barbara Jordan used it to great effect with Cole, whose shouting quickly subsided. She would become well-known for her ability to shrivel an opponent with a few well-chosen words or phrases. No one, least of all her target, will ever forget what she said to a hapless representative of the National Pollution Control Board. Fixing her laserlike gaze upon him, her voice dripping contempt, she demolished him with one sentence: "I have heard your statement, and it is full of weasel words."

Barbara Jordan's amendment was adopted.

The next day she received an official commendation from the Houston City Council because, as Councilman Bill Elliott said, she "demonstrated amazing resistance to pressure and interest in effective pollution control."

Less than a week later Barbara was embroiled in another courageous fight, this time about a new voter registration bill. The bill, sponsored by Senator Tom Creighton of Mineral Wells, would require registration in person rather than by mail and only between October 1 and January 31 and it would require voting applicants to state whether they could write their names and whether they had any physical disability that would prevent them from being able to mark the ballot. In Barbara's view it was a thinly veiled attempt to hamper voter registration by poor and minority people.

"It is alien to the concept that the right to vote ought to be easily accessible and available to all people with minimum details and procedures for registering," she said.

But merely objecting to a bill was not enough to block its passage. She had to marshal a sufficient number of votes against it. In the Senate sixteen votes were required to pass a bill, but twenty-one were needed to bring it to the floor for consideration. The time to block it was before it ever reached the floor. "I opposed it," Barbara recalls, "and needed ten other senators to join me. I made a list of ten senators who were in my political debt. I needed their votes in order to keep the Creighton proposal from Senate deliberation. Armed with ten commitments, I went to Senator Creighton and asked when he planned to bring the bill to the floor of the Senate. He smiled, but with resignation, and said, 'I too can count; the bill is dead, Barbara.' "

Barbara has described what she calls the typical Texas politician as "tough, expansive, and pragmatic." "Lyndon Johnson was the prototype of the Texas politician," she says. She got along well with Johnson and was gratified that he had taken a special interest in her. Several times she was invited to functions at the White House, an honor rarely accorded a mere state senator.

Men like Creighton and Hardeman were also, in Barbara's opinion, typical Texas politicians—"conservative, decent, and practical. I respect them." During her first term in the Texas Senate, Barbara, in turn, earned their respect.

"Her integrity is without question," Hardeman once said. "By that I mean she will never tell you one thing and do something else. She has demonstrated great ability, and she is my good friend."

"She's one of the most intelligent women I've ever met," has been said by so many senators that it is not worth listing their names. At the end of the legislative session, they themselves listed their names in a unique tribute.

On Saturday, May 27, the Texas Senate granted its first black female member an unusual honor. The thirty other senators unanimously passed a resolution congratulating her for her service to the state and for the way she had conducted herself as a freshman senator, and expressing its "warmest regard and affection" to her. The resolution read in part: "She has earned the esteem and respect of her fellow senators by the dignified manner in which she has conducted herself while serving in the legislature, and because of her sincerity, her genuine concern for others, and her forceful speaking ability, and she has been a credit to her state as well as to her race."

Senator Dorsey Hardeman then rose and asked that the names of all senators and the lieutenant governor be added for unquestioned unanimity. Then Barbara was called on to respond.

For the first time in the Senate chamber, and for one of the rare times in her public life, Barbara struggled to fight back tears. She knew how rare was this tribute. She rose to speak, and her voice broke slightly before she regained her famous self-control.

"When I came here on the 10th day of January, you were all strangers. There were perhaps mutual suspicions, tensions, and apprehensions. Now, I believe they have been replaced by mutual respect.

"I am proud to be a part of this body. I consider all of you my friends and I just want to thank you."

The applause was thunderous and prolonged as she made her way around the Senate floor, shaking the hands of each senator. When at last she returned to her seat, she knew without a doubt that she had been accepted by the Texas Senate.

She thought back on the years of work and hope that had been required even to get to the Senate chamber, the times when she was dispirited and wondered whether she should go someplace where it would be easier for a black woman with political hopes. Now, more than ever, she knew it had all been worthwhile. She was glad she had stayed in Texas.

6 Triumphs and Tragedies

Texas was still no southwestern paradise for black people. Discrimination continued in many areas, and being a state senator praised for her legislative work did not exclude Barbara Jordan from some of it. During her first term as a senator she had been invited to speak before many groups—including the Nebraska legislature during a trip there to attend an N.A.A.C.P. convention—and had been honored by a variety of organizations. But when in early May the Austin Club, a private segregated club, decided to hold a party for the Houston delegation, they did so at a time when Barbara and Representative Curtis Graves, also from

Houston, were conveniently "out of town." During the spring 1967 semester T.S.U. had been the scene of student rioting in which a police officer died, many people were wounded, and 488 students were arrested. The facts of the affair were impossible to determine because of the wide variance in eyewitness accounts and the deep animosity between students and police. In both cases Barbara reacted in a characteristically controlled way.

Unlike Representative Graves, she did not publicly express any anger over not being invited to the Austin Club party. And at T.S.U., where she spoke at a Law Day convocation, she told the students that power was not gained by brick throwing but by using judgment and reason.

She was opening herself to a lot of criticism in doing so. In many parts of the country some blacks were putting aside reason. In the summer of 1967 a spate of race rioting erupted in a number of cities. The rioters were primarily poor blacks, for whom the recent voting rights and civil rights laws represented just so many pieces of paper. Such legislation had raised expectations but had not gotten poor blacks better jobs or enabled them to earn more money as a result, so what good were they? Young blacks who had previously participated in the demonstrations to bring about desegregation or who had belonged to S.N.C.C. had come to feel pessimistic and disillusioned and they supported the poor blacks. Leaders like Barbara Jordan were in danger of being shunted aside, just like earlier over-accommodating black leaders, only much more quickly.

Despite pressures to become more militant, Barbara maintained her philosophy that a reasonable, realistic approach was most successful. Late in July she outlined her feelings in a speech before the black National Bar Association:

"We live in a distraught present. Although we have had the courage to deplore it, we have failed to heal the gap between the middle-class black lawyer and the black slum dweller, who hates us almost as much as he hates Whitey. . . .

"We must exchange the philosophy of excuses—what I am is beyond my control—for the philosophy of responsibility. We should tell the citizen that a man of liberty does not burn down the neighborhood store, then beg for his supper. We should tell him that a citizen of dignity does not wait for the world to give him anything."

Her speech drew frequent applause and, when it was over, a standing ovation from the black attorneys assembled to hear her. But from some other segments of the black population it drew accusations that she was "a sellout." She tried not to let either reaction affect her. Her chief responsibility, after all, was to herself and what she thought was right.

In August she donned her "lawyer's hat" and filed suit against the Hughes Tool Company in Houston on behalf of two black employees. The suit charged that the two blacks had been denied the opportunity to advance beyond the lowest and most menial labor grades. In her speech before the National Bar Association she had said the burden of change rested with black lawyers. She was doing her part to bring about change.

In the fall she served as vice-chairman of the Democratic voter registration drive in Texas. She had told T.S.U. students the previous spring "if you don't like the laws, then you withdraw your support of those [representatives] you have selected." She backed up her words with actions, therefore she was respected, albeit grudgingly, even by the most militant blacks.

The voter registration campaign, however, was not particularly successful. Former Mayor Lewis Cutrer was running against Mayor Louie Welch in the mayoralty campaign. The Negro Council of Organizations had endorsed Cutrer, but it never gave any reasons for its endorsement or why it was against Welch. Welch won the November 18th election. Only 38 percent of qualified black voters had turned out to cast their ballots. Overall, only 37 percent of all qualified voters had actually voted—a large black turnout could really have made a difference. But blacks had not felt there was much choice between the two white candidates and so had taken the attitude, "What's the use of voting for either?" That was not, Barbara sighed to herself, the way to make either blacks or whites aware of the black voters' political clout. Perhaps they would do better in next year's election.

But poor blacks, particularly ghetto dwellers, were

not especially inclined to greater participation in the political process. More and more they were beginning to "vote" with bricks and bottles—fed up with the gap between promises and actuality. In March 1968 Barbara was invited to participate in a conference on human relations held at the University of Texas Law School. The conference, which was attended by a number of southern black leaders, discussed, among other things, the rising dissatisfaction in northern ghettos and the possibility that the disorders would reach the South and the Southwest. The participants also discussed the issue of racism. Charles Evers, who would later become mayor of Fayette, Mississippi, stated that in his opinion racism was dead. In the discussions that followed, Barbara disagreed:

"Most Negroes have a little black militancy swimming around in them," she said, "and most white people have a little Ku Klux Klan swimming around in them. If we'd be honest with each other, we would discover we are all victims of [the] racism that is historically a part of this country."

Barbara chaired the closing session of the conference, at which one of the panel members was a Houston attorney named Leon Jaworski. Jaworski had endeared himself to blacks and poor whites in 1965 when he had spearheaded a drive for the establishment of a hospital district with power to levy taxes to support public hospitals. Barbara knew Jaworski; she had participated in various activities within the Houston legal community with him. They would become good friends.

On April 4, 1968, Martin Luther King, Jr., was assassinated, and ghettos across the country erupted in violence. For Barbara, as for so many other blacks, this tragedy, coming just five years after the assassination of John F. Kennedy, was almost too much to bear. What was happening to the United States? It seemed as if the country were dissolving in hatred and violence. Racial animosities, combined with the growing movement against the war in Vietnam, had created such a climate of national strife that it was easy to become dispirited. But Barbara continued to have faith in her country and its political process and to be patient as she waited for the inequities to be ameliorated.

On April 14 memorial services honoring Dr. King were held in Houston as the official end of the period of mourning for the slain leader. Barbara was one of the organizers of the services. She invited Judge Bill Elliott and Mayor Louie Welch to attend: "We search for private and official commitment to the principles for which Dr. King lived and died," she wrote to Welch. "We need your presence to affirm our faith in our future together and in the future of this country."

She frequently found herself called upon to speak about the rising black militancy and the future of race relations in the country. She grew tired of playing the role of spokeswoman for "moderate" blacks. Yet at the same time she believed her voice of reason was needed, and so she tried to accept as many speaking invitations as she could.

"Black Power is a form of withdrawal from the fray—a form of accommodation," she told a group of Texas media people in May. "The whole concept of Black Power acts as a shield of protection from the onslaughts of the society in which Negroes live in America. This concept is founded on fear—absolute, deep, abiding fear.

"The majority of black people in this country, even those who shout the loudest, still believe in white America. The Negro in the main still has faith in your ability to change."

Nineteen sixty-eight was an important election year for Barbara. Because she had drawn a two-year term in the Senate, she had to run for re-election to her seat. She hardly had to campaign—she ran unopposed. More important to her was the presidential election, in which, to her great sadness, Lyndon Baines Johnson would not be a candidate. As he had been popularly elected to only one term, in 1964, he was eligible to run again in 1968. But the war in Vietnam had destroyed him. Blacks, and some whites, realized that on domestic issues, especially in the area of civil rights, he was a great president. But in their violent antiwar feeling many whites and a few blacks forgot this aspect of the Johnson presidency. One day in the spring of 1968 Johnson had delivered an important policy speech on Vietnam. At the very end, to the surprise of everyone but himself and a few close advisers, he announced he would not seek re-election. Barbara was stunned. She feared that the end of the Johnson administration would signal the end of the major advances in civil rights legislation. She also had a more personal reason for missing President Johnson. As one of his protégées she had benefited from having a mentor in the White House. Being invited to functions at the White House had been something of a political plum for her, and just recently, in January, the president had appointed her a member of an elite national panel called the Commission on Income Maintenance Problems, whose other members were well-known economists and businessmen. For a young, ambitious politician it helped a great deal to have the president of the United States take a personal interest in her.

Barbara was a delegate to the Democratic National Convention in Chicago, which would choose the party's presidential candidate. At such conventions it is often customary for a state delegation to vote for a so-called "favorite son" candidate—a state office holder, usually its governor—and thereby withhold its votes at first from one of the major candidates so as to be in a better position to bargain with him or her. Texas Governor John Connally had announced as a favorite son candidate from Texas, and accordingly the members of the Texas delegation were expected to vote for him. Connally was a conservative Democrat, not particularly well-liked by the liberals in his state. Yet in the interests

As a veteran state senator, Barbara Jordan was frequently called upon to act as spokeswoman for moderate blacks.

of state delegation unity most of the liberal delegates were expected to stand behind him, and under a regulation called "unit rule" the delegation was supposed to vote as a unanimous bloc. But Barbara did not intend to do what was expected of her.

"I am going to follow the dictates of my conscience and my constituents," she said. "They do not believe in the unit rule and neither do I. I will not act under it."

"I will not vote for Connally under any circumstances," she stated firmly.

Clearly Barbara was going to be a problem for the Texas delegation, and there was danger that her stand would disrupt the delegation if other liberals followed her example. That danger proved real. Four other liberal Democrats joined her in refusing to back Connally. Certainly the five mavericks presented little threat in terms of numbers—the delegation consisted of 104 members—but their impact on the delegation's hoped-for solid front was considerable.

On Monday, August 26, Barbara was vindicated when the convention voted to discontinue the unit rule. Thus released from casting their votes as a bloc, other, less daring delegates abandoned their support of Connally.

"The defeat of the unit rule means the political leaders will not be able to deliver hand-picked delegations from senatorial districts and conventions to the state and national conventions," Barbara commented.

"It means the people will have to participate in the political process if they want to be delegates to the convention and have their viewpoints represented."

But abolition of the unit rule was a small first step— too late and not enough to satisfy the individuals and groups who felt the Democratic Party did not adequately represent them. For days before the convention began women, members of various minority groups, young people, draft resisters, poor people, and Vietnam veterans had converged upon Chicago in buses and private cars, walking and hitchhiking. Their primary concern was the Vietnam War, but they were also protesting their lack of representation among the predominantly middle-aged, white, male delegates. They chanted; they battled with police; they were beaten, arrested, and jailed. Inside, the convention seemed as if it were under siege; many of the delegates were more concerned, and rightly so, with what was going on outside than with the convention business. As it turned out, so was the country, and the bitter memory of Chicago in August 1968 would haunt the Democratic presidential campaign.

Vice-President Hubert H. Humphrey won the party's nomination, but many of the delegates were unhappy about it. He was a compromise candidate. Conservative Democrats would have preferred a conservative; but since there was no viable conservative candidate, they had voted for Humphrey as a lesser evil than the two liberal candidates, George McGovern and Eugene

McCarthy. Liberal Democrats had favored either Mc-
Govern or McCarthy and considered Humphrey an old-
style politician out of touch with the times. All of the
delegates at the convention could not help wondering
what effect the presence of Robert F. Kennedy would
have had on the outcome. The slain president's younger
brother, Kennedy had made a good showing in the
primaries he had entered. He had represented a blend
of liberalism, government experience (he had served as
attorney general during his older brother's administration), and political expertise that the other liberal
candidates lacked. And he had the Kennedy name and
charisma, an important quality that Humphrey lacked.
Sadly, Robert Kennedy had been assassinated in June,
one more victim of American unrest.

In the balloting at the convention Governor John
Connally displayed an excellent sense of timing in
releasing the Texas delegates still pledged to him from
voting for him as a favorite son. Their votes put
Humphrey over the top, giving him more than the
required number of delegate votes needed for the
nomination. Barbara was satisfied with the Humphrey
nomination. If he became president, he could be
trusted to continue the social programs of the Kennedy
and Johnson administrations—if he became president.

But Hubert Humphrey was defeated by Richard M.
Nixon in the 1968 presidential election. Across the
country blacks and many liberal whites groaned with
dismay. Publicly Barbara said little about the Repub-

lican victory—she was too shrewd a politician to alienate either the new president or his party. Yet privately she was equally dismayed. Republicans were notorious for their lack of innovative social programs and their philosophy that massive government spending on domestic programs was bad for the country.

About the Texas elections she had mixed feelings. The state had a new governor. John Connally had served two terms and was thus ineligible to run for a third. His lieutenant governor, Preston Smith, had been elected. Barbara and Smith had a good relationship based on mutual respect and esteem. She would be able to support many of his programs. The new lieutenant governor and presiding officer of the Senate, Ben Barnes, was a moderate liberal. She would be able to work with him, and she would be able to do so for a full four-year term. Her biggest regret was that Senator Dorsey Hardeman had been defeated in his re-election bid. She would miss him.

There was one more election that November that interested and excited Barbara, not to mention several million other black people. New York Assemblywoman Shirley Chisholm defeated civil rights veteran James Farmer to become the first black woman in Congress. Barbara had to remind herself that New York was New York and Texas was Texas. But rapid changes were occurring in Texas politics, and Barbara's drive to be "outstanding" did not necessarily have to end with the Texas Senate.

7 Rising Political Fortunes

Texas Senator Barbara Jordan started off her first four-year term with a bang. Since all bills introduced in the Senate had to be discussed in committee and reported out first, committee assignments were of major importance. During her previous, two-year term, she had been appointed to all seven committees on which she had sought membership. In her second term she was appointed by Lieutenant Governor Barnes to ten committees. She was made a regular member of eight of them: Education; Finance; Jurisprudence; Legislative, Congressional and Judicial Districts; Military and Veterans' Affairs; Public Health; State Affairs; and

Youth Affairs. She was also made vice-chairman of the Senate Committee on Privileges and Elections. Most important, she was appointed chairman of the powerful Senate Labor Committee.

"Today marks an absolute new era for liberals in the Texas Senate," said Barbara. "I think the lieutenant governor very carefully tried to balance the committees as far as political philosophies were concerned. My appointments are excellent. I received all the appointments for which I had indicated a preference. I did not request a chairmanship, but I was delighted to receive it." Early in the session Barbara was accorded another honor, although it was a somewhat dubious one. The youngest senator serving in the legislative session was honored with a special resolution wishing her a happy thirty-third birthday. The resolution decreed that the "men only" sign in the members' lounge, which adjoined the men's room in the Senate, be removed for that one day.

Barbara proved a strict committee chairman. In fact there was some grumbling among the members of the Labor and Management Committee that she ran it in an almost military style. Meetings started *on time*—and a late-arriving member risked a withering stare and frequently a scornful remark from the chair. Bills were presented, witnesses were heard, discussions were held, and notes were taken in a no-nonsense atmosphere that discouraged down-home jokes or back-slapping techniques. When the meetings were adjourned, they were

over—few lingered around to engage in small talk.
Yet, operated in this way, the committee was highly productive. Under her chairmanship the committee reported out both a minimum wage bill and a bill to
increase workmen's compensation benefits to workers
injured on the job. And through her clever political
maneuvering Barbara played a major role in seeing
that those bills were passed.

There was plenty of opposition, especially to the
minimum wage bill. Texas had never had a minimum
wage law before, and a few die-hard conservative
senators staged a filibuster to prevent a vote on the
proposed bill before the legislative session ended. Yet
the bill, which would set the state minimum wage at
$1.25 an hour as of February 1, 1970, and at $1.40 a
year later, was finally passed after a last-minute compromise exempting business firms employing fewer
than five persons and farmers hiring fewer than four
workers in any one quarter of the year. The workmen's
compensation bill was also a compromise bill agreed
upon by the Texas AFL–CIO, the Texas Manufacturers
Association, and the Texas Trial Lawyers Association.
In fact the three lobbying groups had written the bill,
without consulting the legislature, which made some
legislators angry. The bill also granted benefits that
were lower than the national average for workmen's
compensation, which angered other legislators.

Both bills were too strong in the opinion of some
and too weak in the opinion of others. For the first

time Barbara was aware that behind her back liberal legislators were accusing her of "selling out." She tried not to let those accusations bother her. The workmen's compensation bill might not be perfect, but labor, management, and trial lawyers had battled each other to a standstill over the issue for the last twelve years. The minimum wage bill might not be as generous or as all-encompassing as it could be, but it was the first such law ever to be passed in Texas. Imperfect though they were, they were better than no laws at all. She refused to be unduly affected by adverse criticism from her colleagues. She looked instead to the working people she had promised to represent. They cheered her. And she took heart from the following statements made in the Houston *Chronicle* on June 1:

"The 61st Legislature enacted the state's first minimum wage law and greatly improved benefits for injured workers.

"These were the session's two major achievements in the field of labor-management legislation."

Coming from the Houston *Chronicle*, a traditionally conservative newspaper, that was high praise indeed.

It was and continues to be difficult for a black leader to follow his or her own convictions without being criticized by one group or another. There are still few leaders who are black, and because that is so, they are expected to answer to blacks of every political and economic persuasion. It is almost an impossible task. Every stand or opinion will be disagreeable to some.

The militants demand militancy, the moderates a more conservative approach. What is good for the ghetto dweller is not necessarily beneficial to the black middle class, and yet the leader is expected to represent the best interests of both groups. A black leader is automatically exposed to the criticism that he or she is forsaking one or the other of these segments of black society. It can be extremely unsettling to be branded a militant and a sellout on the same day and over the same issue. The successful black leader must not take such criticisms to heart and must proceed in the manner he or she thinks best.

Barbara's way was usually the middle path, neither radical nor extremely conservative, a steady liberalism that made her attractive to people with a wide range of political views. She was inundated with guest-speaking requests and accepted a remarkably large number of them considering the huge amount of legislative work she had. The Texas legislature is notorious for its numerous committees—it has more standing committees than even the United States Congress. Barbara's committee load was one of the largest in the Senate.

In addition she served on various nonlegislative committees. In February 1970 she was named to the environmental health committee of the Southern Conference of State Governments. In March Governor Preston Smith appointed her to head an interim study committee to look at programs for the handicapped in Texas. She was already on the Senate Interim Committee for Urban Affairs. In July she added the Senate Interim Committee on Election Law Study to her list of assignments.

Meanwhile she attended to the affairs of her regular Senate committees, holding hearings and presenting resolutions to improve the Texas judicial system, to raise the ceiling on welfare benefits, to improve health services to the poor, to offer disadvantaged youth greater educational opportunities at community colleges, to increase employment opportunities, to consolidate the various social services offered by the state and its communities. By now, "If you want something done, get Barbara to do it," had become an often heard maxim. What dedication, considering that her salary as a senator was a miserly $4,800 a year!

Because she was such a "doer," Barbara was able to say a lot of things to her audiences that they would not take from other speakers. The makeup of her audiences didn't seem to matter. In April 1970, when she spoke before a group of blacks in Huntsville, Texas, she admonished both those under thirty and those over thirty:

". . . Young people must learn to sit at conference tables with their elders, instead of going out and blowing up the Capitol," she said.

"Wear an Afro haircut if you will, that is your choice. But under that haircut there is nothing other than a black American. You were not born in Africa, so you're not Africans."

95]

Those over thirty she chided for "standing on the sidelines watching the world destroyed. . . . You will get what you deserve suffering the clock turned back unless you find your voice." And as for black militants: "They say that hate and violence are necessary. I ask them, 'What are you doing to save our country?' "

Sometimes militants would argue with Barbara, pointing out the inequities to which blacks were still being subjected and asking how to do away with them without violence. One of the situations that particularly rankled Texas blacks was the comparatively small number of black elected officials in the state. As of April 1970 Texas had only twenty-nine such office holders, lower than any other state in the South. In Mississippi and Alabama, where voter registration drives had led to murder and other violence, the numbers of black elected officials were eighty-one and eighty-eight, respectively. Houston, with a large black population, did not have a single black on its city council. These statistics bothered Barbara Jordan, too, but she preferred working for change within the system to the sort of violence that had scarred other areas of the South. Texas might be slow to change, but it was changing nevertheless, and as the top black elected office holder in the state, Barbara found it difficult to complain personally.

Nineteen-seventy was another important election year in Texas, and the Democratic Party decided to stage an all-out drive for victory that would put aside factional disputes between liberals and conservatives in favor of the common goal of getting Democrats, no matter what their politics, elected. Governor Preston Smith decided that the time to start displaying this unity of purpose was at the State Democratic Convention in September. He announced that he intended to nominate former Lieutenant Governor Ben Ramsey, a conservative, as convention chairman and Barbara Jordan, a liberal, as convention secretary.

Ramsey, however, was a bit too conservative to be a wise choice. When he had served as lieutenant governor back in the 1950s, he had been staunchly segregationist and antilabor. To liberal and labor Democrats he was unacceptable, and they said so.

Barbara found herself in a difficult position. She wanted to serve as convention secretary, but to serve in that capacity with Ramsey as chairman would be hypocritical. She informed Governor Smith that she would not accept the job of convention secretary if Ramsey held the gavel. If he insisted on keeping Ramsey, there would probably be a showdown vote at the convention, which would surely destroy the uneasy harmony then prevailing among the various factions of the party. Smith relented, Ramsey's nomination was withdrawn, and Barbara became convention secretary.

"This is the first time a black person has ever been named an officer of this convention," Barbara told a cheering crowd. "I think it is past due.

"All of us remember the times we couldn't even get

a seat at this convention. That day is over. . . ."

One more first for Barbara Jordan. Her list of firsts was very impressive by now. Although they primarily involved Texas, they were beginning to bring her to national attention. In December she was named by *Harper's Bazaar* as one of "One Hundred Women in Touch with Our Time" and described as the "most potent, influential voice in the state for blacks . . . a gifted, able orator."

Soon political and population changes in Texas would pave the way to increased national attention for her. Nineteen-seventy was a census year, and the increase in the population of Harris County that had occurred over the past decade would almost certainly create the need for a fourth U.S. congressional seat for the county. If a fourth seat in Congress was warranted, liberal Democrats were prepared to push for another redistricting of the county that would create a congressional district out of the black, Mexican-Americans, and poor white precincts surrounding Houston. Such a district would be tailor-made for a liberal Democrat with a good record on integration and programs for the poor. State Senator Chet Brooks, State Representative Curtis Graves, and Harris County Judge Bill Elliott all had expressed interest in the creation of such a new district. And no one had to ask if Barbara Jordan was interested. It would be perfect for her, and she had made it known she would like to move up to Congress.

Early in 1971 Barbara found out that she had been

one of the targets of an army spying operation in Texas. Walter Birdwell, a twenty-eight-year-old Houston postman, came forward with the information that while he was attached to the 112th Military Intelligence Corps from 1965 to 1967, he had attended meetings and demonstrations and taken notes on who was present. The army's chief interest had been in people who were against the war in Vietnam, and Birdwell had paid particular attention to members of Students for a Democratic Society at the University of Texas and to the heads of various committees against the war. But he had also collected information on Muhammad Ali, whose refusal to serve in Vietnam had cost him his world heavyweight title; Representative Curtis Graves; and Senator Barbara Jordan.

Barbara had made a number of antiwar speeches, but needless to say she had never regarded herself as an enemy of the country. According to Birdwell her file in the Federal Building at Houston had been only one-quarter-to-one-half-inch thick, which indicated the army had been unable to find much "on" her. Yet the very idea that such spying activities were going on disturbed her. More disturbing than her personal discomfort was the idea that the Bill of Rights, which guarantees individual liberty and privacy, was being subverted.

The disclosure of the army's spying on her did not affect Barbara's legislative work. She was as busy and as productive as ever. In February she was co-sponsor of a bill to add an amendment to the state constitution that would guarantee equal rights for women; it was unanimously passed by the Senate. Later in the month she introduced bills that would create a fair employment practices commission and require that all publicly funded contracts include provisions against discrimination. She also introduced a bill to establish a department of labor in the state. In March she sponsored bills to create a state department of human affairs and to establish a nonprofit corporation to make loans for low-income housing. And in April a bill she sponsored to create a state department of community affairs was passed in the Senate. But as the spring wore on, she concentrated on the pending congressional redistricting, the need for which, as expected, had been shown by the results of the 1970 census.

As mentioned earlier, if a new district could be carved out of the poor and primarily minority wards near downtown Houston, several Houston officeholders would be in a position to benefit. In the Senate those officeholders were white liberal Democrat Chet Brooks and Barbara Jordan; and when it came time for Lieutenant Governor Barnes to choose the members of the subcommittee to study redistricting and draw the boundary lines of the new district, both wanted to be on it. One made it. Barbara Jordan was not only named to the panel, she was appointed vice-chairman.

At the end of May Barbara formally recommended a redistricting plan that involved the entire state, wherever population changes required district changes.

In Houston her plan did not unduly disrupt the districts of the three U.S. congressmen already serving in Washington; they would be able to run safely in them again. But the new fourth district was made up of just the people she had so ably represented in the Texas Senate. It was perfect for her. Early in June both the House and the Senate approved the bill. The following year, 1972, the first U.S. representative from the new, 18th Congressional District would be elected.

There were grumblings from some legislators about the results. Barbara Jordan had ordered up a congressional district for herself, and it had been served to her on a silver platter! But even the grumblers had to admit to her political cleverness. She had managed it all without threatening the re-election hopes of the three Houstonians already in Congress.

Congressional elections were a year away, but the idea that Barbara Jordan would be the newest Texan in Congress was already set in the minds of many. That may be one reason why she found herself the subject of special honors in the fall of 1971. To be sure, she had earned the respect and admiration of many in the state, but it is also likely that some of them were rushing to get a front seat on the Barbara Jordan bandwagon.

At the end of September Mayor Louie Welch proclaimed Friday, October 1, as Barbara Jordan Appreciation Day in Houston. But the major testimonial came toward the end of October, when former President Lyndon B. Johnson headed a list of leaders honor-

Lyndon Johnson supported Barbara Jordan throughout her career.

ing her as "the epitome of the new politics in Texas."
Among the others were Lietenant Governor Ben Barnes;
Mayor Louie Welch; and her old debating team part-
ner, Otis King, who had since become dean of the law
school of Texas Southern University.

There were many speeches. Barnes called Barbara
"the person who worked hardest for single-member
districts and worked hardest to make sure Ben Barnes
stood up for single-member districts in Harris County."
Welch called her a "responsive" legislator "who was
responsible for legislation to make Houston, Dallas,
and the municipalities in Texas better places to live."

But of course the most important words to be spoken
came from Lyndon Johnson: "Barbara Jordan proved
to us that black was beautiful before we knew what it
meant," he said. "Wherever she goes, she is going to be
at the top. Wherever Barbara goes, all of us are going
to be behind her."

Barbara thanked Johnson. "You made us all feel like
first-class Americans," she said, "and we all enjoy
feeling that way."

As to where she was going, there was little question
in anyone's mind, least of all Barbara's. Her only
regret was that she would not be the first black woman
to sit in the U.S. House of Representatives. "I do not
view with any great favor being only the second black
woman elected to Congress," she said. "I would like to
have been the first, but Shirley Chisholm beat me there.
I would like to join her."

8 Barbara Jordan for Congress

It was fortunate for Barbara that congressional re-districting occurred when it did, enabling her to plan to run for election to the U.S. House of Representatives rather than for re-election to the Texas Senate. Under the redistricting plan Houston state senate districts had also been altered, and the way the new district lines were drawn it would be very difficult for a black to win in Barbara's old 11th District. It had been redrawn to include approximately the same percentage of blacks (38 percent), but the whites it now included were not the blue-collar, working-class whites of the old district; they were middle-class whites, who shared fewer common interests with blacks. They would be less likely to vote for a black candidate. Also, it now included areas already represented by incumbent white Senator Chet Brooks, who would be a difficult opponent for a black Senate hopeful. Testifying before a court hearing on the redistricting in a suit brought by State Representative Curtis Graves, Barbara said even she probably couldn't win re-election to her old seat. Of course, she wasn't planning on seeking re-election, a situation that Graves pointed out. "I am fully cognizant of the fact that this district was carved out for Senator Barbara Jordan and that she already has begun a campaign," Graves had said back in the summer of 1971.

At that time Graves also decided to seek election to the U.S. Congress from the newly created 18th District. Two of the very few black officeholders in Texas running against each other for the same office was not in the best interest of black politics in Texas. It might split the black and liberal vote in the district. But in politics, as in most other areas of life, it's everyone for him or herself. When the Harris County Democratic Party, a liberal organization, met to make its endorsements in late March 1972, it avoided a split in its ranks by giving Jordan and Graves dual endorsement.

Both Jordan and Graves lived in Houston. Both espoused liberal Democratic causes. Both had been elected to the Texas legislature in the same year and shared the distinction of being among the first three blacks to serve in the legislature since Reconstruction.

Beyond these similarities the two had little in common. Graves was a native of New Orleans and had attended Xavier University there before moving to Houston. He had received a degree in business administration from Texas Southern University and worked as a public relations consultant before being elected to the Texas House in 1966. In 1969 he was an unsuccessful candidate for mayor of Houston. Married and the father of three children, Graves had an outgoing personality. Early in his first session in the Texas House the pageboys had named him representative of the week. His wardrobe included a fire-engine red vest.

Barbara was quieter, more subdued. She commanded respect more than outright friendship; it took time for people to get to know her well. And although she didn't object to a fire-engine red vest, she herself dressed conservatively.

Graves was emotional and not ashamed of it. "I cried the morning I was sworn in," he said. "I realized it wasn't a dream anymore. It was reality. I realized a whole segment of history was over, and a new segment was beginning."

Barbara kept her emotions under tight rein. Only once, back in 1967 when she'd been named outstanding freshman senator, had she nearly broken down. The quiver in her usually strong voice had occasioned comment in the newspapers, for it was a rare occurrence. Charlotte Phalen, a Houston *Post* reporter, once related to Molly Ivans, then a Washington *Post* reporter, an anecdote that revealed the extent of Barbara's self-control: Phalen had invited Barbara to her home for a game of poker and Barbara had accepted, although because of her strict Baptist upbringing she was hardly accustomed to playing cards. "You know how most people who've never handled a deck before will drop the cards all over and fumble around? Not Barbara. She gripped each card firmly and carefully set it down in front of each player. Not one of those slippery little things was going to get out of her control."

Curtis Graves was highly outspoken. In the spring of 1967, after he had sat in session in the Texas legislature for some two months, Graves was asked what he thought of his fellow black representative, Joseph Lockridge. "He's just sprayed black," Graves said. "He doesn't think black." By contrast, when asked how he felt about Graves, Lockridge had said simply, "I have made his acquaintance. He is competent." In August 1971, when he expressed his intention to run for the 18th Congressional District seat, Graves had this to say about Barbara: "Senator Jordan has demonstrated a blind loyalty to the Democratic Party machine. . . . [She] has seldom involved herself in anything controversial, let alone anything controversial concerning the black community."

Barbara Jordan always spoke in measured words, appealing to reason, stating the facts. In response to Graves's criticism that August she had stated simply: "The representation of black people does not have as

a necessary prerequisite involving oneself in controversial issues. In my judgment black people want representatives who can get things done for them. . . . I
am quite willing to offer myself to the black community
on the basis of my record of performance."

With two such distinct personalities opposing each
other, the race for the Democratic primary election in
May promised to be a lively one.

Graves formally announced his candidacy early in
February, and in a speech at T.S.U. he made clear that
his campaign would be largely based on his contention
that Barbara had "sold out" her constituents: "I feel
now, more strongly than ever, that the congressman
from this new district must be someone who owes his
allegiance to the people who live in the district, not
to the corrupt politicians who have brought our state
into national shame and ridicule," Graves said.

"If you are looking for someone who goes along to
get along, one who plays politics with your lives, one
who is long speaking, but short on delivering services,
then don't vote for Curtis Graves."

Throughout the campaign Graves would stress the
"sellout" issue; and the press, always interested in
controversy, printed his charges, giving him good publicity. But Barbara got more press coverage. Although
some of it was not directly related to the campaign, it
was most helpful to her candidacy.

It was customary periodically throughout the year
for the Senate to elect a president pro tempore to serve

as assistant to the lieutenant governor, the presiding officer of the Senate. Whoever occupied that position automatically became third in line of succession to the governorship; it was the highest office the Senate could give. With the convening of a special session of the Senate in late March, the election of a new president pro tem was one of the first orders of business.

The Senate usually rotated the job on a seniority basis, but this time there was not one but eight senators next in line—Barbara and seven others had all come to the Senate in the same year. But it was no contest. Sixteen senators rose to give seconding speeches to her nomination, and she was elected unanimously. Their remarks indicated just how highly her colleagues regarded her.

"It is a high compliment, and I speak for all of us when I say we are proud of you," said A. M. Aiken, senior senator.

Senator Roy D. Harrington expressed amazement at the amount of work she had been able to accomplish: "She has been able to get more legislation through than most of us."

Senator Ralph M. Hall, a conservative, and often her enemy on legislative matters, praised her, too: "She must command our respect for her work for those who have no lobby."

And Chet Brooks called her "one of the finest human beings I have ever known."

A beaming Barbara Jordan rose to be sworn in and

delivered a brief acceptance speech: "When I came here January 10, 1967, we were all strangers. Now, on March 28, 1972, I am enjoying the friendship and fellowship of this body. Nothing can happen in my lifetime that can match the feeling I have for my service in the Texas Senate, and nothing that can happen to me in the future will be greater than receiving this high honor right now."

By mid-April the primary candidates were campaigning hard. The streets of the 18th Congressional District were papered with posters—VOTE FOR BARBARA JORDAN—VOTE FOR CURTIS GRAVES—and few automobile bumpers escaped being adorned with campaign stickers. Barbara's campaign material was of a higher quality than Graves's. The print on his leaflets faded quickly and wasn't properly aligned. Being a public relations consultant, he was disturbed by the unprofessional look of his material, but there was nothing he could do about it. He didn't have the money Barbara had. She was getting $5 in campaign contributions for every $1 he received.

Barbara's campaign was being financed by whites, Graves charged. Downtown whites were supporting her in "an open attempt to buy the first black congressman from the South." According to Graves the money Barbara was receiving was being contributed in return for Barbara's having helped redraw the state Senate district lines in a way that would prevent another black from being elected to the Senate for the next ten years.

Barbara replied that when the list of contributors to her campaign was made public, as required by law, "it will clearly show there is no faction or select group financing my bid for election."

As to Graves's charges that she had deliberately re-drawn the Senate district lines to exclude black rep-resentation in the legislature, Barbara stated, "The drafting of the Senate redistricting bill was done by a legislative redistricting board. I had nothing to do with that board."

Sometimes it seemed to Barbara that she was spend-ing half her campaign time and money responding to Graves. She had enough to do without constantly re-stating her answers. Campaigning was exhausting activity, although Barbara never seemed to show her tiredness. On a typical day, for example, she was at her law office at 8 A.M., opening her mail and answer-ing telephone calls. By 9 she was at her first campaign stop, a union headquarters, shaking hands, making a brief speech, answering questions. She concentrated on her record in the Texas Senate—the number of bills she had introduced and the number that had been passed, the ways in which she had helped poor and working people. She contrasted her record in the Senate with that of Graves in the House—only one of the bills he had introduced had been passed. Sometimes she couldn't resist an obvious pun and would refer to "the

Barbara campaigning

Graves we are going to dig on May 6," but as a general rule she refrained from making personal remarks about her opponent.

On to her campaign headquarters to see how the supply of leaflets and bumper stickers was holding out, then lunch and another campaign stop, this time at a vocational high school. "The society which scorns plumbing because plumbing is a humble activity and tolerates shoddiness in philosophy because it is an exalted activity will have neither good plumbing nor good philosophy," she told the students. "Neither its pipes nor its theories will hold water."

Pleased with her reception at the school and with her speech, she hummed as she drove back to her headquarters. She enjoys music, and when she isn't listening to it on the radio, she hums to herself. After an hour or so directing operations at her headquarters, she got back into her car and set off for another appearance, this time at a housing development. Traffic was heavy. She let a Cadillac move in front of her.

"Lady," she said, "my name is Barbara Jordan and I am running for Congress. Don't forget that I let you in."

She visited a supermarket; she spoke to a group of beauticians at a church; she appeared at a meeting of Oil, Chemical and Atomic Workers. She shook hands but rarely back-slapped. She smiled at babies but didn't kiss them.

It was late in the evening when she returned home.

While eating the supper her mother had kept hot in the oven for her, she told her parents briefly what her day had been like. Then, exhausted from the day's activities, she got a few hours' sleep. Late in April a reporter asked her how she managed such a hectic schedule. She smiled. "Some nights you crawl into bed and you think, 'What is it I'm really doing?' "

On Saturday, May 6, a large number of Democratic voters turned out at the polls, and by midafternoon early reports showed Barbara had a commanding lead over Curtis Graves.

"They're stealing the election from me," Graves complained, "but I can't prove it. I can't get any poll watchers."

Barbara did not respond to these new charges of Graves's.

By evening it was time for Barbara's victory speech. Final results would show that she had won 80 percent of the vote and had carried black, Mexican-American, and white sections of the 18th District.

"Back in December when I entered this race, I promised to represent all the people of the 18th District, black, white, brown, young and old, rich and poor," she told her cheering supporters. "Nothing has happened in this campaign to change that resolve. Instead, I have received support and votes from all those groups. It is widespread support that has enabled me to win today, and I'm deeply grateful for it."

She did not say much about Graves except that she

considered their contest unfortunate because "Houston's black community can't afford to lose any leaders." Later, though, both she and Graves would come to feel that perhaps their contest had contributed to the political education of Houston's black voters. "It has brought a maturation of the black voter," she said. "He has to look at the person and say, 'What can he or she do for me?' Whites have been doing it for years, but the black voter is just now changing his voting pattern from habit to the issues.

"When I first ran for the legislature in 1962, the black voter didn't know what the legislature was supposed to do," she continued. "With my election to the Senate and Curtis's election to the House came a new awareness. Now you couldn't find a black in Houston who doesn't know something about the legislative process."

The celebrations at her campaign headquarters lasted far into the night, and by the time she got to bed, it was 5:30 Sunday morning. At 8:30 she was up and slogging through the rain to Good Hope Missionary Baptist Church, where, after services, the church ladies honored her with a tea that lasted four hours.

Back home the phone rang. Barbara sighed and picked up the receiver.

"Hate to be a nuisance, but I—" said the voice on the other end.

Barbara cut the caller short. "Yes," she said, "I am very tired."

The worst was over, however. Opposition from her Republican opponent in the November election would be token at best. She was already talking about how she would act in Congress.

"I'll go there with as much in-depth knowledge as possible of the issues that concern people and move into that body in a way most effective to get things done. I want to get in motion and attend to the concerns of the people of the 18th District."

It would be nine months before she took her seat in Congress. She still had her Texas Senate term to finish. And before she assumed the job of congresswoman, she had another office to hold—that of "Governor for a Day."

9 Governor for a Day, and Congresswoman-Elect

A traditional custom in Texas was for both the governor and the lieutenant governor to leave the state for a day, allowing the Senate president pro tempore a day as governor. A week after the Democratic primary it was announced that both Governor Preston Smith and Lieutenant Governor Ben Barnes would be out of the state on June 10. That would be Barbara's day as governor.

Immediately Barbara was placed in a difficult role because she was black—and she was placed in this position by another black. Back in 1968 Lee Otis Johnson, who had gained notoriety during the civil rights disorders at Texas Southern University in 1967–1968, had been sentenced to thirty years in prison for giving a marijuana cigarette to an undercover police officer. Many black people had felt that that was an unduly harsh sentence and that Johnson had not received a fair trial because of the unfavorable climate of opinion in Houston at the time. When it was announced that Barbara would be governor for a day on June 10, a black activist named Ovide Duncantell decided to ask her to pardon Johnson. He made his announcement on the lawn in front of her law offices, on a day when she was out of town.

The issue was soon laid to rest. Returning to Houston, Barbara responded to Duncantell's request by pointing out that only the State Board of Pardons and Paroles could grant Johnson a pardon. "Not even Preston Smith himself could now grant Lee Otis Johnson an executive pardon," she explained. She handled the matter well—with reasonable arguments devoid of emotional content. But it had been an insult just the same. It was hard enough contending with whites without having to be on guard against her own people.

The press called it "History in One Day," but it had taken Barbara Jordan a lot longer than that to arrive at the position of influence in Texas politics that enabled her to become "governor" and thus the only black woman in United States history ever to preside over an entire state (if only for one day). But all the work and frustration had been worth it, she decided, as she passed through lines of cheering spectators on her way to the Capitol building at 9:30 on the morning of Saturday, June 10.

Inside the Senate chamber her fellow senators rose to applaud her, and the galleries burst with smiling well-wishers. With her mother and father beside her she took the oath of office on the platform that held the Senate's chief executive chair, a platform somewhat altered in appearance for this one day. Only five of the traditional "Six Flags over Texas" were in place. The flag of the Confederacy had been removed. "I didn't issue any proclamation or edict requiring the flag to be removed," Barbara said later. "I think those in charge felt it would not be proper for a governor of . . . this race."

After she took the oath, Leon Jaworski, now president of the American Bar Association, spoke. Some of his remarks would prove to be prophetic:

"We are proud of you on this day, as we have been on other days; and may you, for the benefit of the society that is ours, continue to lead us to achievement of the greatest of all goals of good citizenship—that of forming a more perfect union."

Barbara had been part of a movement sponsored by the American Bar Association to give students a better understanding of the duties and obligations of citizenship. Said Jaworski, "The greatest compliment we could pay Governor Jordan on this day is to give our unstinting support to this endeavor in the Texas schools. . . . she believes in the processes of a democracy, upholding the standards that made this country great and deploring those that would erode its greatness."

The speeches over, the spectators gave her another standing ovation. A reception and press conference were scheduled next. As she hugged her parents, Barbara noticed that her father did not look well. His heart condition had forced him to retire even from his activities as a minister in January, at the age of sixtynine. He was just tired from the morning's excitement, he assured her. Would she mind if he did not go to the reception? He would just go out to the car and rest awhile.

Barbara and the rest of her family made their way to her office, where she spoke to reporters and greeted the hundreds of people who had come to see her sworn in. A barbecue luncheon was to be held on the Capitol grounds and an afternoon ceremony was to be held on the Capitol steps.

At about 11:30 Barbara's brother-in-law, John McGowan, took Reverend Jordan to the hospital. He had suffered a stroke. Barbara asked about his condition and was told it was "satisfactory." So she remained in the Capitol, executing her largely ceremonial duties as "Governor for a Day."

She signed three proclamations, one of which praised the work of the Sickle Cell Disease Research Foundation. Sickle cell anemia is an inherited blood disease found almost exclusively in blacks. "Governor" Jordan declared September "Sickle Cell Disease Control Month" in Texas. The other proclamations praised the work of the Texas Commission for the Blind and the City of Austin. She was also handed a proclamation from Mayor Welch of Houston declaring the day as "Governor Barbara Jordan Day" in Houston. Some observers pooh-poohed the whole affair as a publicity stunt, but that didn't bother Barbara. She kept her sense of humor, which nearly always contained a serious note. "Someday I may want to retain the governor's chair for a longer period of time," she said.

Reverend Benjamin M. Jordan died about twenty-four hours after he was admitted to the hospital. Although she was saddened by her father's death, Barbara was thankful that at least he had lived to see her sworn in as Governor for a Day. From the time she had been able to understand the concept, he had encouraged her to be as much as she could be, and he had worked very hard to finance her education. He had lived to see his efforts rewarded. In a way, she told a friend, it was beautiful that he had died at just that time.

The Jordan family established a Reverend B. M. Jordan Memorial Scholarship Fund. All his life he had emphasized "brain power," and he would have been pleased to be remembered in this way. One of the trustees of the fund was Leon Jaworski.

One week after Barbara's day as governor five men

were caught breaking into and bugging the Democratic National Committee Headquarters at the Watergate complex in Washington, D.C. There was little question that the "plumbers," as the group called themselves, had been working for the Committee to Re-elect the President, and some people suspected that high officials in the Nixon administration had authorized, or at least known about, the break-in. The FBI began an investigation of the Watergate affair, but its investigation was limited to the men who had been directly involved, and calls for a more in-depth investigation were ignored.

Back in Texas Barbara's day as governor had completed her term as president pro tempore of the Senate. She was succeeded by her friend Chet Brooks, who was elected to the position for the special session of the Senate that convened in mid-June. It would be Barbara's last session. Autumn was fast approaching, and with it the November elections.

In September she received another honor. Democratic gubernatorial nominee Dolph Briscoe wanted a black person in a high Democratic party post, either as vice-chairman of the State Democratic Executive Committee or as a Democratic national committeewoman. As the most politically prominent black person in the state, and a woman besides, Barbara was the logical choice. She became the first black vice-chairman of the State Committee, a position which automatically gave her a half vote on the National Committee.

Above: *Barbara Jordan, Governor for a Day.*
Below: *Barbara with Presidential nominee George McGovern*

The Democratic National Convention of 1972 was very different from that of 1968. Back in 1968 many groups that had no voice in national politics had protested, violence had erupted, and the image of the party had been tarnished. But changes had been made in the process of delegate selection in the intervening four years, and when the 1972 convention opened there were more female, minority, and young delegates than ever before. The majority of them supported Senator George McGovern of South Dakota for the presidential nomination, because he had pledged to end U.S. involvement in Vietnam, to introduce programs that would benefit the poor, and generally to speak to the issues they thought were important. Barbara supported McGovern. He was designated the Democratic Party's candidate; and though he faced a tough campaign against President Nixon, he and his supporters had faith that through his fine character, his deep religious conviction, and the sincerity of his wish to help the people who needed help, he would win.

McGovern's nomination proved to be the high point of his campaign; from then on it went steadily downhill. In response to persistent rumors Senator Thomas Eagleton, McGovern's choice for vice-presidential candidate, revealed to McGovern and the press that he had been hospitalized for "nervous exhaustion" three times in his life. The revelation was followed by questions about his mental stability. The press was full of stories about it. Fearing that a Democratic ticket that included

Eagleton would lose the election in November, Mc-
Govern decided after some delay to take Eagleton off
the ticket. R. Sargent Shriver, McGovern's seventh
choice, agreed to be his new running mate. It will
never be known how the Eagleton candidacy would
have affected the Democrats' chances. It is known that
many people were disappointed in George McGovern
for not standing behind his first choice for vice-
presidential nominee. Many had been first attracted to
him because he seemed different from most politicians.
In changing running-mates, he seemed to be putting
political considerations over human considerations,
just like other politicians. Other voters felt McGovern
was just too liberal, even radical, too closely associated
with minorities and youth.

The Democrats tried to make the Watergate break-in
a campaign issue, but the general attitude of the country was that it had been an isolated occurrence, that
such activities were common among both Democrats
and Republicans, and that President Nixon had been
unaware of the plot. In the November election many
Democrats crossed party lines and voted Republican,
and Richard Nixon won by a landslide.

In Texas Barbara Jordan also won by a landslide,
capturing 80 percent of the vote against her Republican
opponent, just as she had done in the May Democratic
primary against Curtis Graves. She and Andrew Young
of Georgia, also elected that year, would be the first
black representatives from the South since 1901; Bar-

bara would also be the first black Congress*wo*man from the South. "I feel great," she said.

A month later she would indicate just how good she felt and just how self-confident she was. In mid-December she spoke at a civil rights symposium marking the opening to researchers of former President Lyndon Johnson's civil rights papers. "Texas has done a lot for this country," she said. "It has given you Lyndon Johnson, and now we've given you Barbara Jordan."

She was proud of her victory and proud of her record during her terms in the Texas Senate. She had seen about half the bills she introduced enacted into law, including a Texas Fair Employment Practices Commission, the state's first minimum wage law, and an improved workmen's compensation act. She had backed successful measures to strengthen environmental protection laws and to create a special department of community affairs to deal with the problems of the state's growing urban areas, and she had prevented passage of a discriminatory voter registration act. She believed she had truly represented the people who had elected her and earned the respect even of those who hadn't, and she felt her large vote total in the general election proved her belief was correct. "If I got 80 percent of the votes, lots of white people voted for me," she said shortly after the election, "and it was because they felt their interests would be included."

There were those who disagreed with her assessment

of her senatorial achievements. Curtis Graves was not the only one who called her a "sellout," although he was clearly the most vocal. Some liberal senators felt she had hurt their cause:

"I'd carry a bill on some problem, a strong bill," said one. "Barbara would carry one too, but it would be weak. And it would get through. The trouble with passing a weak bill is that you won't get another crack at strengthening it for twenty-five–thirty years. Whereas if you just hold firm, you'll get a tough one through, this session or next. It was great for the establishment to have her on their side. Whenever we tried to do anything, they could say, 'But Barbara doesn't think it needs to be that strong, and if *Barbara* doesn't think so . . .' "

There was also the controversy over whether or not she had had to "cooperate" with conservatives in order to get the new 18th Congressional District drawn the way she wanted it. Reporters, always interested in controversy, frequently brought up these charges, although it was a rare reporter who ever brought them up more than once. Barbara would flatly deny them, and as reporter Molly Ivans once wrote, "When Jordan denies something in her weighty, absolute fashion, even the most persistent reporter doesn't feel like bringing it up again."

After the November election Barbara didn't stay around long to give press interviews. Harvard University, which sixteen years before had refused to accept a poor black girl from a small all-black southern college, had named her a fellow at the Institute of Politics of its John F. Kennedy School of Government. She would be one of four newly elected representatives in an experimental, month-long "cram course" designed to prepare them for their new lives as members of Congress. In addition to Barbara another Texan, Alan Steelman, and another black woman, Yvonne Braithwaite Burke of California, were taking the course. The fourth new member was William Cohen of Maine.

The curriculum ranged from informal lectures on how to choose an office and file a bill to briefings on major issues. The four engaged in mock debates, as if they were speaking on the House floor, and early on Barbara called attention to a problem female representatives faced. According to rules of congressional decorum, legislators had traditionally referred to a colleague as "the gentleman from Massachusetts" or "the gentleman from Utah." With the entrance of women into Congress the term had to be changed and "gentlelady" had come into use. "May I object to being called 'gentlelady'?" asked Barbara during one of the seminars at Harvard. "How would you want to be addressed?" asked her fellow Texan, Alan Steelman. "I don't know, but I don't like 'gentlelady,'" Barbara answered. One suggested solution was for Barbara to make a brief speech early in the congressional session to make her wishes known. But after thinking the matter over, Barbara decided such a speech would be petty and would call negative attention to the fact that she was a woman in a body in which the overwhelming majority were men. Though she would never be happy with it, Barbara resigned herself to being called "gentlelady." She would become famous as the "gentlelady from Texas."

10 First Year in Congress

Barbara Jordan was not completely immersed in her studies at Harvard between November 1972 and January 1973. She was busy arranging for the furnishing of her office in the Rayburn House Office Building and finding a place to live. (She invited her mother to come to Washington to live with her, but Mrs. Jordan preferred to remain in Houston.) She was also trying to select a Washington staff and a staff to take care of her business in Houston while she was in Washington. In this, as in most other things, she did an excellent job; her staff is among the most efficient of the congressional staffs around and has been instrumental in helping her build her own reputation for efficiency and preparedness. And finally, she was beginning her drive for membership on the House Committee on the Judiciary.

Barbara wanted to be on that committee. When asked why, she said it would complement her legal background and deal in legislation important to the problems of her district (it was a major checkpoint for civil rights legislation). Shortly before the 93rd Congress convened, former President Lyndon B. Johnson telephoned Representative Wilbur D. Mills of Arkansas, then chairman of the powerful House Ways and Means Committee, which made committee assignments for all Democrats, and expressed his hope that Barbara would be appointed to the Judiciary Committee.

The 93rd Congress convened on January 3, 1973. Along with other new legislators Barbara took the oath of office from House Speaker Carl Albert. About one hundred supporters from Texas witnessed the ceremony. They had come on a plane specially chartered for the purpose. After the House session a reception for Barbara was to be held in a committee room in the Longworth House Office Building.

The first session of the 93rd Congress was not long, but there was some business to conduct. A Speaker of the House had to be elected. Representative John Conyers of Michigan, head of the Congressional Black Caucus, made a token bid for the job, but Carl Albert from Oklahoma had seniority and was the favorite. Barbara voted for Albert.

Barbara also received a job, one that usually goes to a freshman member, that of secretary of the Texas delegation. The vote was unanimous with the exception of her own. She voted for herself as chairman!

Barbara was late for her party. After the formal session on the House floor she had sought out New Jersey Democrat Peter Rodino. Rodino was slated to be named chairman of the Judiciary Committee, and of course Barbara wanted to put in her bid to be on it. For his part Rodino wanted to get Barbara on the committee, because he could use her support in his largely black district in Newark, New Jersey. Traditionally two representatives from Texas sat on the committee, and since one Texas seat was vacant . . . Arriving late at the party given for her, Barbara was cheered when she explained she had been on the floor of the House "working for them."

Most of the other representatives from Texas were at the party, as well as some representatives from non-southern states. Barbara took charge of introducing her fellow congressmen to the crowd.

"And there's Representative Burleson," she said as she stood on the platform and peered over the heads of the crowd, "a charming man I earnestly want to introduce to you. He's a member of the House Ways and Means Committee and consequently will have a lot to say about my committee assignment."

The crowd laughed, and so did Burleson. "And she'll get whatever she wants," he said to those around him.

A week later Barbara had her committee assignment.

On January 22, 1973, former President Lyndon B. Johnson suffered a fatal heart attack. Aware of the mutual respect and admiration Johnson and Barbara had for each other, a reporter called Barbara that night. The Barbara Jordan who answered the telephone was not in very good control of herself. In a grief-stricken voice she said, "I think history will record Lyndon Johnson as one of the greatest presidents this country has had."

Barbara would never forget Lyndon Johnson or what he did for her and for black people. "Old men straightened their stooped backs because Lyndon Johnson lived," she once said. "Little children dared to look forward to intellectual achievements because he lived. Black Americans became excited about a future of opportunity, hope, justice, and dignity because Lyndon Johnson lived.

"He was my political mentor and my friend," she added. "I loved him. And I shall miss him."

Over the next few months Barbara missed Lyndon Johnson more and more. President Richard Nixon seemed to be doing his best to undermine the social programs of which the Johnson administration had been so proud. Proposed cutbacks in the new federal budget included money for health, welfare, housing, urban development, sewage treatment plants, and community projects. With two other representatives from the Houston area Barbara held hearings in Houston to find out just how the cutbacks would affect the people of Houston. What they learned made the legislator resolve to fight the cutbacks wherever possible.

Meanwhile Barbara was concerned that the government belt-tightening seemed to be hurting most the people who could afford it least. "Why wasn't Nixon also talking about reducing subsidies?" she asked. She was equally concerned that the senior Democrats in the House seemed to be unwilling, or unable, to stand up to the president. After all, there was a Democratic majority in the Congress. Quietly Barbara and the other first-term Democratic representatives came together in an informal caucus to act as a catalyst in convincing Congress to resist the will of the White House. In April, after the House failed to override two Nixon vetoes on spending measures, Barbara and another freshman Democrat, Edward Mezvinsky of Iowa, decided to defy the tradition that freshman members are traditionally seen and not heard. "In the ninety days that I've been in Congress," said Barbara, "I find that Congress is having difficulty finding its back and its voice." She and Mezvinsky decided to ask for four hours' time on the House floor in mid-April for the freshmen to make their plea. They went to see Speaker of the House Carl Albert to discuss their desire to prod the House into reasserting its authority. Albert seemed compliant. To each point the freshmen raised, he said, "Fine." But Barbara sensed that he really wasn't paying much attention to them. Finally Barbara exploded

U.S. Representative Barbara Jordan

and told the Speaker that it wasn't all "fine." "The inability of the Democratic majority to decide on a course of action and to move on it . . . has caused a deep sense of depression, not only among freshmen, but among some of the most senior members of Congress," she said. More serious in Barbara's mind than the depression of Congress was the imbalance between executive and legislative branches of the government that threatened the most basic parts of the Constitution.

The freshmen's opportunity to speak came a week later. In the interim two of the Texas Democratic freshmen pulled out of the program, complaining that the original idea of discussing the budget control problem had "exploded" and the caucus had become labeled as both anti-administration and anti-House Democratic leadership. Undaunted, Barbara remained in the program, and in her remarks on the House floor on April 18 said that the nation faced "one-man rule" on federal spending and "inaction in the Congress."

"As freshmen members of Congress, we have a unique perspective on this," she said in her speech. "We are here because the American people voted against monolithic government in the 1972 elections. They clearly wanted some restraint on executive branch power and they hoped to get it by electing Democrats to Congress while a Republican president maintained control of the White House."

As freshmen, she said, she and her colleagues didn't expect to wield a great amount of power in Congress, but "we do not expect powerlessness of Congress as an institution."

Powerlessness was a frustrating problem for the freshman congressmen in the 93rd Congress. So were the rules, the bureaucracy, the rigamarole, that attended the legislative branch of the U.S. government. The rules were not as arcane as those of the Texas legislature, but the political interests were more complex and more numerous. The Texas legislature had debated issues that concerned Texas; in the Texas Senate there were only thirty-one voices to be heard. The U.S. House of Representatives was composed of people who represented a much broader political spectrum and made decisions affecting the whole country. And there were so *many* representatives, each highly aware that they came up for re-election every two years and thus were impelled to *produce,* even if his or her production was just words. To many freshman congressmen the situation was strange, frustrating, and sometimes ludicrous, and they were drawn to each other as a consequence of both their powerlessness and their incredulity.

Barbara Jordan and Charles Wilson formed a close relationship that spring. Both were from Texas, and they had served together in the state Senate. Politically they differed at times—but they both shared the same feeling about the process of government in the nation's capitol. It was pompous, wasteful, and sometimes funny.

"Charles and I never take ourselves seriously, but we

both work very hard," Barbara said that spring. "We get so tickled at the folks who act as if they were in sole control of the ship of state. We can't resist sticking a pin in such puffery just between the two of us."

Wilson said of Barbara, "She's one of the few real people in a profession that is known for its phonies. I have a high regard for her because she is a no-nonsense person who votes compassionately and tries to do for her people. But she doesn't wear it on her sleeve. She's not a grandstander."

Barbara was equally complimentary of Wilson. In the House the tall, lanky white man and the tall, heavy-set black woman came to be called "the odd couple," but not derisively.

"They've got the right idea," said a fellow member of the Texas delegation. "They get as much done as the rest of us and yet they'll probably escape the ulcers bit. You might as well enjoy public service if you can."

Wilson was one of the Texas freshmen who had declined to participate in the attempt by Barbara and other first-term congressmen to "wake up" the House of Representatives. Barbara told him it was his first real chance to stand up to the president and he had muffed it. He smiled and told her jokingly that he was a tool of the administration.

It is unlikely that the speeches by Barbara and the other freshman Democratic members of the House made any major impact, although they did establish the fact that the freshmen did not intend to be silent, as they were traditionally expected to be. Richard Nixon continued his one-man rule, and during the months that followed, it seemed that he might soon be the one man in his original administration left in the White House.

In January the five Watergate burglars and the two men accused of directing their operations had been brought to trial, and all had been sentenced to prison terms. All had remained silent and declined to take the witness stand in their own defense, which had further aroused the suspicions of many that people in high places had known about the burglary. Judge Sirica, who presided over the case, said publicly that he was "not satisfied" that all the facts had been brought out and he urged a congressional inquiry. Shortly afterward, on February 7, the Senate created a Select Committee on Presidential Campaign Activities, headed by Senator Ervin. In addition, many members of the press voiced suspicions. Their reports and articles kept the Watergate affair before the American public and maintained pressure on the Nixon administration. Events began to move swiftly as new facts were brought to light. On April 30 John Dean, counsel to the president, was fired, and John Erlichman, assistant to the president for domestic affairs, and H. R. Haldeman, chief of staff at the White House, resigned because of their involvement in the Watergate affair. At the same time, Attorney General Richard Kleindienst resigned because of his closeness to the people now under investigation.

This was Barbara's reaction: "The question remains: Is this enough? Does this really take care of all the wrongdoers? I will reserve my judgment until we see whether this cleans house or not."

Within a few days it became apparent that the "house" was not "cleaned." John Dean was busily leaking stories all over Washington about the Watergate scandal and hinting that President Nixon himself had been involved in trying to cover up White House involvement in the burglary. The special Senate committee began its televised hearings on May 17 to investigate the matter, and on May 22 the new attorney general Elliott Richardson appointed Harvard law professor Archibald Cox as special prosecutor to handle an independent investigation.

Much of the credit for uncovering the relationship between the Watergate burglars and the White House belonged to the press, particularly the Washington *Post*. Barbara Jordan praised the press publicly for doing so. Now, perhaps, Congress would reassert its authority and regain its constitutional powers from the control of the president.

"We have learned that we cannot allow excessive delegation of power to go unchecked," she said. "Today I am very hopeful that some of the money [frozen by Nixon] for education and health care will be restored by Congress."

But the Watergate scandal and its repercussions seemed to overshadow all other activity of the legislature. On October 30, 1973, the special prosecutor for Watergate, Archibald Cox, was fired by the president. Cox had been promised complete independence; but after it had become known that Nixon had for years ordered all his office and telephone conversations taped, and Cox had subpoenaed those tapes that he felt were relevant to Watergate, he was fired. As a result Attorney General Elliot Richardson and his deputy, William Ruckelshaus, resigned.

All of this happened on the same day. The press called the affair "the Saturday Night Massacre." Barbara told reporters she thought the firing of Cox was "a serious intrusion into the administration of justice." Of Richardson and his deputy aide she said, "Their resignations remind us that it has become difficult for men of conscience to serve President Nixon. It is a tragedy that we have to constantly remind this president that there are certain principles of justice which are embodied in the traditions and laws of this country."

In Congress it was proposed that there should be a special prosecutor truly independent of the president. Nixon had said he would appoint a new special prosecutor, who would have "independence and total cooperation" from the White House, but many members of Congress believed any special prosecutor under direction of the White House could not really be independent. Barbara was one of them. In testimony before the House Judiciary Subcommittee on Criminal Justice she called upon Congress to authorize the U.S. Court of Appeals to appoint a new special prosecutor.

"In a sense we ask too much of this administration," she said. "When the executive branch is both defendant and prosecutor, we should not expect either dispassionate inquiry or vigorous prosecution."

She introduced a bill into Congress that would permit federal grand juries to ask district judges to appoint special prosecutors during investigations of officials of the executive branch of government.

Before the bill could be acted upon, Acting Attorney General Bork appointed a new special prosecutor— none other than Leon Jaworski, Houston attorney. Jaworski's terms for accepting the appointment were stiff. The president could not fire him except for "extraordinary improprieties," and he must be guaranteed the right to sue in court for presidential tapes and other evidence.

Politics is a small world, thought Barbara upon hearing the news. Now her old friend Leon Jaworski was special prosecutor. She believed he would be a fair and independent one—he would not bow to administration wishes.

Discussion by the House Judiciary Subcommittee about the office of special prosecutor was tabled. There was other serious business to attend to. Early in October Vice-President Spiro Agnew had resigned, pleading nolo contendre (no contest) to charges of Federal income tax evasion. In the House it was the job of the

Judiciary Committee to hold confirmation hearings on the president's new appointee.

Gerald R. Ford was a Republican from Michigan who was well-liked in Congress. Barbara Jordan agreed that he was a personable man, but that didn't qualify him for the vice-presidency. In the confirmation hearings she came down hard on his civil rights record. Asked about his stand on civil rights, Ford declared that every American is entitled to equal treatment. "I've lived that, I believe that, I insist on that," he said.

Barbara was not convinced. She recalled that Ford had once said in a speech, "In politics, when the train is moving, you'd better jump on because you don't get a second chance."

Would it be fair, she asked, to characterize his voting record on civil rights as "trying to stall the train as long as you can and then jumping on when you know it will keep on going no matter what you do?"

Ford said he disagreed. Barbara fixed one of her famous stares on him. He shifted uncomfortably in his seat.

The questioning of Ford was rugged—so rugged, in fact, that Barbara predicted a Nixon resignation in mid-1974. "It was evident that in the minds of many of the members was the unspoken thought that Mr. Ford would be president and that its job was really confirming the next president of the United States," she said.

Barbara, for one, didn't believe Ford was qualified.

When the Judicary Committee voted on his confirmation, hers was one of the eight dissenting votes. Now
Ford's appointment would go to the full House for a
vote.

The Judiciary Committee voted on Gerald Ford on
December 1, 1973. Three days later Barbara was hospitalized for tests. Lately she had been feeling a numb-
ness in her arms and legs—she obviously had some sort
of infection in the nerve endings in her limbs. She had
begun feeling the sensation—which was similar to the
feeling one gets when one's foot goes to sleep—on
November 29. Doctors at the hospital decided to keep
her there for a week.

That meant she would be unable to vote when the full
U.S. House of Representatives decided on the confirmation of Gerald Ford as vice-president. Her absence
bothered her. So far during her first term she had
voted 99 percent of the time, the highest record of
voting participation among members of the Texas
delegation, and the ninth highest record among members of the entire Congress. Her vote would not have
made a difference, however. On Thursday, December 6,
Gerald Ford was confirmed by a sizable majority of the
House.

On Saturday, December 8, Barbara left the hospital.
Doctors there had been unable to discover the cause of
the infection. But at least they had ruled out cancer,
tumors, and other serious causes. She was back at work
on Monday, and her colleagues in Washington seemed

pleased that she was. The Senate Ladies (wives of senators), however, were a bit miffed. They had sent her flowers while she was in the hospital, and they had never received a thank you by word or note. Barbara was getting a reputation in Washington for such discourtesies. It wasn't that she was rude, really—cold was the word most often used.

Late in December Congress recessed and Barbara had an opportunity to look back on her first months in the U.S. House. She described the experience as not exactly frustrating but one that had "required tremendous patience on my part at times." It also required a great deal of work. By the time she reached her southwest Washington apartment at night, she had time only to fix dinner for herself, skim through the legislative business for the next day, and fall into bed. She hadn't time for the round of cocktail parties for which Washington was famous. Her life was her work.

Yet she was glad she was in Congress and pleased with her performance, although she had necessarily been limited because she was a freshman. She was proud of her 99 percent voting record and of her part in the attempt by freshman Democratic representatives to "wake up" the Congress to President Nixon's "one-man rule" over federal spending. She was also pleased that the American Conservative Union had rated her voting record on major issues the lowest of the Texas delegation. But she was most pleased with her membership on the House Judiciary Committee, which in the next year seemed certain to consider whether President Nixon would be impeached. Perhaps the most important constitutional question of the century would be decided, and she would be a part of the process.

Hearings on impeachment were sure to be held, and Barbara had become reticent about Nixon since her prediction that he would resign. She was deeply aware of her responsibility under the Constitution that she regarded so highly.

"If I was convinced now that Mr. Nixon is guilty of a crime worthy of impeachment, then I ought to disqualify myself," she said to anyone who asked. "An impartial investigation demands an open mind and I intend to keep one."

11 The Impeachment Hearings

On January 12, 1974, Barbara announced that she would seek a second term in Congress and would run in the May Democratic primary. But this time there was no Curtis Graves to oppose her. In fact there was no one at all to oppose her. She was grateful for the lack of opposition, for it enabled her to devote her time to her activities in the House.

It was a busy spring. The energy crisis had become a reality to Americans, and there were massive oil shortages across the country. Barbara introduced a bill that would require oil companies to turn over information on all their activities to the government's General

Accounting Office. She also predicted that product shortages, rising prices, and the energy crisis would result in the creation by Congress of a consumer protection agency. In February she co-sponsored with Representative Martha Griffiths a bill that would provide social security coverage to homemakers, a group that had traditionally been denied benefits because their work was done inside rather than outside the home.

Meanwhile, as a member of the House Judiciary Committee, she was busy hearing testimony and receiving evidence on the twenty-two articles of impeachment that had been introduced into the House after the Saturday Night Massacre and referred to the committee. At the end of 1973 Committee Chairman Peter Rodino had appointed Wisconsin Republican John Doar, former head of the Justice Department's Civil Rights Division under Presidents Kennedy and Johnson, as the committee's counsel. Doar saturated the committee with evidence, and there were many nights when Barbara sat up until dawn reading pages of testimony. Yet she would not have traded her committee assignment for any other. "It is impeachment or the prospect of it that undergirds everything that's done in the House right now," she said in March. "If I weren't on this committee, I'd feel like an outsider in the House, because those who are not on the Judiciary Committee don't really know where we are with regard to impeachment, or what the plans are, or where we intend to go."

On March 1 a special grand jury handed down an indictment against former presidential aides H. R. Haldeman and John Erlichman and recommended that certain material reportedly damaging to the president be forwarded to the Judiciary Committee. That material included some tape recordings of presidential conversations, and after listening to them John Doar believed he had a case for impeachment. But to make a solid case he needed more tapes. So did Leon Jaworski. Both men asked the White House for forty-two additional tapes. The White House refused; President Nixon would not give up any more tapes. The Judiciary Committee was just conducting a "fishing expedition," he charged.

Barbara publicly disagreed. "We are seeking six conversations related to the Watergate coverup," she said, "and they are on forty-two separate tapes. It's not our fault if these people are long-winded."

And she took issue with the president's claims that "executive privilege" enabled him to withhold the tapes. "Before impeachment, executive privilege falls," she said. "Before impeachment, confidentiality falls. And impeachment is the one exception to the separation of powers."

Such speeches were gaining her considerable renown in Washington circles and earning her renewed respect at home. That week a highly laudatory article about her appeared in *The Christian Science Monitor*. One of the politicians the article quoted was Louisiana

Democratic Representative John L. Rarick, one of the House's most conservative members and an old-line segregationist, who called her "the best congressman Texas has got."

She did not act exclusively like a black, a woman, or a liberal, but "like a representative in Congress," said Rarick.

A week later she was praised by Speaker of the House Carl Albert himself. His remarks came at a fund-raising dinner honoring Barbara in Washington, at which he predicted that she would one day be chairman of the Judiciary Committee. "It's the safest bet you can make in politics," he said, "whether or not the House seniority system survives in its present form.

"She came to Congress in her thirties; she'll be there in her sixties. She has the head, the heart, and the muscle to make her kind of democracy count."

Barbara was pleased with the praise, but she felt the need to qualify Albert's predictions: "I may be in the House of Representatives till I'm sixty-eight," she said, "but I may want to move on to someplace else before that time. I want to be there [in Congress] as long as I want to be there."

A few weeks later Albert asked Barbara to preside over the House in his absence. Those who had heard the Speaker make his prediction about Barbara chuckled that if he did not watch out she would have *his* job.

Meanwhile the members of the House Judiciary Committee continued their investigation into the impeachment of the president; as the evidence against him mounted, a subtle change began to occur, and the committee members began to come together: "When we began to sift through this whole morass, this mountain of information, that is when it all began to jell," Barbara later recalled. "I can't point to any specific revelation which caused the mood of the committee to shift, but around mid-April the partisan acrimony was reduced. People started to listen and look and make decisions."

On April 11 the House Judiciary Committee voted, thirty-three to three, to issue a subpoena for forty-two additional tape recordings. A week later Special Prosecutor Leon Jaworski issued a subpoena for sixty-four additional recordings. Barbara, among others, hoped that the president would comply with the subpoenas. "Realistically there is no way for the committee to enforce its subpoena. We are not going to have the specter of the sergeant-at-arms or the doorkeeper or the security counsel for the committee trying to seize the president."

Yet, in Barbara's view, if Nixon did not surrender the tapes, his refusal itself might be considered an impeachable offense.

She was called upon to give her opinions on the matter publicly often that spring. She appeared on the *Today* show and on the news program *Issues and Answers*. In May she was one of the two members of the Judiciary Committee chosen to discuss the matter of impeachment on the Public Broadcasting System. She was getting more national publicity than probably any other first-term member of Congress.

Some Republican congressmen criticized her for speaking so openly about impeachment, but Barbara did not let the criticism concern her. She was much more concerned about the erosion of traditional liberties that she felt the whole Watergate affair had brought out into the open. The American people had to be made aware of the situation, and she made them aware at every opportunity.

She had agonized over the impeachment question: "I have the same high regard for the office of the president as the majority of Americans. He is a figure who towers above all other figures in the world. Certainly no one could seriously consider forcing the president to leave office before his term expired. This feeling stayed with me a long time." But the evidence had mounted, and reluctantly she had concluded that impeachment was unavoidable if the Constitution was to be preserved.

She had originally been "left out" of the Constitution, and yet she had seen how the provisions of the Constitution had been flexible enough eventually to include her. She had great reverence for the Constitution. Twice she had gone to the National Archives and stood in line with the other tourists to view that document. She had stared down at the yellowed parchment pages and realized anew how important it was to the country—and to her. She thought about the Constitution a lot those days. Sometimes she mentioned it. When she referred sarcastically to the suspicious gaps in the tapes Nixon had surrendered, she said, "There are no gaps, there are no inexplicable 'hums,' in the Constitution of the United States."

"We know that liberty is shaky because modern technology now has invested the government with the tools to invade private affairs through certain kinds of electronic mechanisms," she said in a commencement address at Harvard University. "Thomas Jefferson warned us that the natural process of things is for liberty to yield and government to gain ground. . . .

"In recent years we have witnessed a willingness to accelerate the erosion of these guiding principles of American life. The erosion is very insidious because it didn't happen all at once, but one step at a time.

"It happened under the guise of law and order. This erosion of civil liberties happened under the guise of the maintenance of national security; it happened . . . under the guise of executive privilege."

By the middle of July the House Judiciary Committee hearing of arguments and evidence on the impeachment of the president were about to conclude. All that remained were the final arguments by Special Prosecutor Leon Jaworski, Committee Counsel John Doar, and James D. St. Clair, the president's own lawyer. On Thursday, July 18, St. Clair concluded the president's impeachment defense, and he did so in surprising and alarming fashion.

*Barbara with House Judiciary Committee Chairman
Peter Rodino and Committee Counsel John Doar*

The committee had previously subpoenaed the tape of a March 1973 conversation between the president and his former chief of staff, H. R. Haldeman. The White House had refused to surrender the tape, claiming it was not relevant. On July 18, 1974, St. Clair suddenly produced a 2 ½-page transcript of a portion of that taped conversation, claiming that it disproved the allegation that Nixon had authorized the payment of money to convicted Watergate burglars E. Howard Hunt and G. Gordon Liddy.

The committee was flabbergasted, and many were outraged at St. Clair's audacity. How dare he wait until the "eleventh hour" to release a portion of a tape no one outside the White House had seen! How dare he present as evidence a 2 ½-page, edited transcript of a one-hour-and-twenty-four-minute conversation!

"I couldn't believe it, I couldn't believe it," Barbara said, shaking her head. "It focuses on the utter contempt the president holds for the House of Representatives."

Even some of the Republicans on the committee, who wanted to give the president the benefit of every doubt, were forced to reconsider their stand on impeachment.

On the evening of Wednesday, July 24, the House Judiciary Committee began its televised debate on the impeachment of President Nixon. The thirty-eight members sat in two tiers of black leather chairs, the senior members on the top tier, the freshmen and other junior members on the lower level. Before each were piles of documents, for as many as twenty-two articles of impeachment had been proposed. These were some of them:

> Obstruction of justice in the Watergate coverup and approval of hush money and executive clemency for Watergate defendants.
>
> Nine charges of bribery, a specific impeachable offense under the Constitution.
>
> Unlawfully wiretapping citizens and creating the "plumbers" to undertake "covert activities without regard to the civil rights of citizens."
>
> Misusing the Internal Revenue Service to harass political enemies.
>
> Violating the Constitution by receiving federal money in excess of compensation by law; specifically money spent on his homes at San Clemente, California, and Key Biscayne, Florida.
>
> Committing fraud by underpaying his income tax between 1969 and 1973 by nearly $500,000.
>
> Contempt of Congress and the courts by refusing to comply with subpoenas for materials for the impeachment inquiry and Watergate trials.
>
> Concealing from the Congress facts concerning the existence and extent of bombing operations in Cambodia in the spring of 1969.

Lying to Congress; specifically his firing of Special Prosecutor Archibald Cox on October 20, 1973, "in abrogation of commitments to the United States Senate and to the people of the United States." [The White House had promised that Cox would have complete independence.]

The committee had decided to consider three main articles, on lying, covering up, and abuse of executive power, with two minor articles on bombing operations in Cambodia and tax evasion. According to the rules they had set, each member of the panel would be permitted to debate them for fifteen minutes. The statements began with that of Chairman Peter Rodino and proceeded according to the arrangement of the panel, the top tier first. Having convened at 7:45 P.M., the committee adjourned at 10:40 that night; Barbara's turn to speak would come the next day.

The committee reconvened at 10:10 A.M. Thursday, July 25. Methodically the speeches continued, and yet they did not drone on. The members of the committee were all highly aware of the historic significance of the hearings and of their own responsibility. Those who supported the president demanded facts—"specificity" became a catchword in the hearings. Those who were against the president gave those specifics, emphasizing different acts that they considered impeachable offenses according to their own viewpoints.

Barbara too could have listed those offenses she

considered impeachable. Well-prepared as ever, she could recite dates, conversations, and so on, as well or better than any of her fellow members. But her speech would not be comprised of a string of meticulously researched quotes from the White House transcripts. Her speech would deal with tough interpretations of broad constitutional issues and the concept of due process. More than anything else, it would focus on her feeling that *her* Constitution was being subverted.

At 8:15 P.M. the committee reconvened after its dinner recess. Charles B. Rangel, Democrat from New York and one of the three blacks on the panel, spoke. Then Joseph Mariziti of New Jersey delivered his speech. Then Chairman Rodino said, "I recognize the gentlelady from Texas, Ms. Jordan, for the purpose of general debate, not to exceed a period of fifteen minutes."

"Thank you, Mr. Chairman," said Barbara. "Mr. Chairman, I join my colleague, Mr. Rangel, in thanking you for giving the junior members of this committee the glorious opportunity of sharing the pain of this inquiry. Mr. Chairman, you are a strong man and it has not been easy, but we have tried as best we can to give you as much assistance as possible.

"Earlier today we heard the beginning of the Preamble to the Constitution of the United States. 'We, the people. . . .' "

It was a long speech, taking up nearly the entire fifteen minutes allotted to her. But none of her listeners fidgeted. Her voice was hypnotic, her words powerful, and by the time she had said, early on, "My faith in the Constitution is whole, it is complete, it is total. I am not going to sit here and be an idle spectator to the diminution, the subversion, the destruction, of the Constitution," she held her audience captive.

"I heard her on the radio," said a friend, "and I thought it was God."

She spoke of specific presidential acts, but she concentrated more on the precedents for impeachment as specified in the Constitution and as applied during the one earlier impeachment proceeding the country had seen, that of President Andrew Johnson. To her mind there was no question that the president's acts warranted impeachment, for ". . . a president is impeachable if he attempts to subvert the Constitution.

"If the impeachment provision in the Constitution of the United States will not reach the offenses charged here, then perhaps that eighteenth-century Constitution should be abandoned to a twentieth-century paper shredder. Has the president committed offenses and planned and directed and acquiesced in a course of conduct which the Constitution will not tolerate? That is the question. We know that. We know the question. We should now forthwith proceed to answer the question. It is reason, and not passion, which must guide our deliberations, guide our debate, and guide our decision."

With that speech Barbara Jordan became a national

figure. Through the medium of television millions had watched and heard her and had been overwhelmingly impressed. Blacks and women, in particular, were proud to claim her, but the appeal of her dignity, her articulateness, her concern, transcended racial and sexual lines. Her photograph was featured in both *Time* and *Newsweek* that week. The Washington *Post* carried the complete text of her speech the next morning on its editorial page, the only Judiciary Committee member's speech to be carried in full.

On Thursday night, July 25, the House Judiciary Committee concluded the first round of its landmark impeachment debate, and it was almost certain that impeachment would be recommended. Of the thirty-eight members, nineteen had declared their belief that Nixon would be impeached and five other members had indicated pro-impeachment leanings.

The opening debate concluded, the committee now went into more intensive debate. Some of the Nixon supporters on the committee charged, as they had earlier, that they had yet to be shown where the president had specifically committed an impeachable offense. Other members of the committee again tried to point out the specifics. The president's supporters then complained that he had been denied due process of proper notice in the committee's impeachment proceedings. By 6 P.M. Saturday Barbara was visibly irritated. They had been conducting this intensive debate since Friday morning. At 8 P.M. Saturday evening, when the committee reconvened after dinner, she asked to speak. Her remarks were scathing:

"It apparently is very difficult for the committee to translate its views of the Constitution into the realities of the impeachment provisions. It is understandable that this committee would have procedural difficulties, because this is an unfamiliar and strange procedure. But some of the arguments which were offered earlier today by some members of this committee in my judgment are phantom arguments, bottomless arguments. Due process. If we have not afforded the president of the United States due process as we have proceeded through this impeachment inquiry, then there is no due process to be found anywhere. . . . Due process? Due process tripled. Due process quadrupled. We did that. The president knows the case which has been heard before this committee."

On the evening of Saturday, July 27, the first article of impeachment came to a vote. The committee had heard evidence and debated on the matter for months; and while they were relieved to be voting at last, none of them, including the staunchest opponent of the president, was happy about what had to be done. With the eyes of millions of Americans fixed upon the faces of the committee, the clerk called the roll:

Mr. Donohue—"Aye"

Mr. Brooks—"Aye"

Mr. Kastenmeir—"Aye" . . .

On and on the voices droned. There were tears in the

eyes and lumps in the throats, and votes cast in self-conscious voices.

Mr. Drinan—"Aye"

Mr. Rangel—"Aye"

Ms. Jordan—"Aye," said Barbara in a low voice.

The vote was twenty-seven to eleven; Article I of the impeachment resolution had been adopted. Chairman Rodino recessed the committee until Monday morning. Spectators in the room went wild; reporters tried to corner the committee members. Barbara, like many others, wouldn't talk at all as she hurried from the room. Later she said, "There were tears behind doors and off camera after the vote, from both men and women."

By Wednesday, July 31, three articles of impeachment had been adopted by the committee, and two had not been. These last two, dealing with the bombing of Cambodia and the president's questionable financial dealings, were supported by Barbara, but she was relatively satisfied with the three articles that had been adopted. She was more than satisfied with the way the committee had conducted its six-month probe. It had gained the respect of even the strongest Nixon supporters. And once again she, like many Americans across the country who had never really thought about it before, marveled at the strength and resiliancy of the Constitution, which provided the framework under which the crisis that faced the nation could be handled in dignified and orderly fashion. The rule of law had been reaffirmed.

The vote of the House Judiciary Committee was just one step in the impeachment process. Its verdict would be reported out to the full House, which would then vote on whether or not to impeach the president. If the House did vote to impeach, a trial would be held in the Senate. It was quite possible Barbara would be a part of that trial, for there was speculation around Washington that Chairman Rodino would choose her as one of the five or six "managers" of the impeachment case in a Senate trial should the House approve impeachment.

The matter never came to trial in the Senate, nor was it ever voted on by the full House. On the evening of Thursday, August 8, Richard M. Nixon resigned. Vice-President Gerald Ford became president of the United States.

There seemed no rest for the House Judiciary Committee. Immediately they began confirmation hearings on President Ford's choice of a new vice-president. Barbara voted with the majority to confirm former Governor of New York Nelson A. Rockefeller. In her opinion Rockefeller would provide balance to the administration, tempering Ford's "classic conservatism."

She was beginning to think better of Ford now than she had when she had opposed his confirmation back in December of 1973. She was pleased with his first speech to the nation as president and gratified when, on August 21, he invited the Black Congressional Caucus to meet with him at the White House. She found him open to their suggestions and willing to work with them. "Even more important," she said after the meeting, "he told us to just pick up the phone and call him. If he wasn't in, the call would be returned. And we believed him." Such an invitation would never have come from Richard Nixon.

Within a week Barbara had also gone to the White House as a female member of Congress, and shortly thereafter the president invited her to be part of a congressional delegation that would visit mainland China, the only freshman member on the trip.

During her entire time in Washington under the Nixon administration Barbara had been invited to the White House only twice.

But just as she was beginning to like Ford, he acted in a way that caused her to revert to her original opinion. While Barbara was in China, President Ford pardoned former President Nixon, making him immune from any criminal prosecution.

"I think President Ford acted prematurely in not letting the process of the administration of justice work before interspersing his presidential decision," she said after she returned from the trip.

There were calls for an investigation of the pardon, and Barbara agreed that such an investigation should be held. But there was not enough support for the idea in Congress. The legislators, and many of their constituents, were tired of the whole matter. For over a year the country had been subjected to one shock after another—John Dean's testimony implicating the president in the Watergate coverup, the resignations of Haldeman and Ehrlichman, the resignation of Vice-President Agnew, the firing of the first special prosecutor Archibald Cox, and the resignation of the attorney general, Elliot Richardson, the endless exposure of the president in his own lies—and there was a strong urge to return to some kind of normalcy. But suspicions about the pardon would linger, and now the case against Nixon could never be closed. The dangling threads of the Watergate scandal offended Barbara Jordan, along with other Americans who wished the Constitution had been followed to a final conclusion.

On the bright side, however, Barbara was much more confident now of the ability of the Congress to maintain its constitutionally authorized check on the executive branch. The House Judiciary Committee had done its job well, and there was no question that everyone involved in the impeachment process who had approached it seriously and sincerely had benefited from the experience. They had learned a lot; most important, perhaps, they had learned something about themselves. They had also benefited from it politically (only Charles Sandman of New Jersey, the most strident Nixon supporter on the House Judiciary Committee, would be hurt, losing his bid for re-election to the House as a near-direct result). Leon Jaworski, who had insisted on his independence as special prosecutor and pushed relentlessly for the Nixon tapes, was no longer a well-known Houston attorney but a nationally famous lawyer. In October he received the third annual award from the Barbara Jordan chapter of the Susan B. Anthony Society, because he had "made a maximum effort to sustain the American system of justice while it was under attack from many quarters."

Clearly, however, no one had benefited more than freshman Congresswoman Barbara Jordan. She had captivated the press and a large segment of the American public. Washington's Main Public Library offered videotapes of the Judiciary Committee's televised hearings, as well as former President Nixon's farewell address and President Ford's swearing-in. A spokesman for the library said in October, "More people have requested Jordan than any other speaker."

The conservative weekly magazine *U.S. News & World Report* called Barbara one of the Democratic Party's "new luminaries" and quoted an unnamed observer as saying, "When the Democrats get around to nominating a black on their national ticket, they may well turn to Barbara Jordan."

But for the time being, Barbara was content to return to Congress for a second term, and in November Houston's 18th Congressional District re-elected her over her Republican and third-party opponents by a whopping 84.7 percent.

12 A Freshman No More

The price of being well-known for getting things done is being given more to do. Barbara Jordan knew that only too well. The more she had accomplished in the Texas Senate, the more committee assignments she had been given. Now the same thing was happening in the U.S. House of Representatives.

In December 1974 new committee assignments were announced. In addition to serving on the House Judiciary Committee in the new, 94th Congress, she would also be on the Government Operations Committee. This appointment pleased her, as the G.O.C. had been her second choice—after the Judicary Committee. She was

also appointed to a ten-person Democratic task force
assigned to draft an "action agenda" for House Democrats to pursue in the new Congress. Then, too, she
would be serving on the Democratic Compliance Review Commission, whose responsibility was to enforce
the party's antidiscrimination rules and to assure full
participation of all groups in party affairs. And she
was appointed by Speaker Carl Albert to be one of
the three "at large members" of the new Steering and
Policy Committee of the House Democratic Caucus, the
first black woman to serve on the increasingly influential committee that had taken over the responsibility,
formerly held by the House Ways and Means Committee, of appointing Democratic members to the standing committees of the House.

"You should see how everybody, including the old
rednecks who've been running things in Washington for
decades, are now bowing and scraping to Barbara,
since she's one of those with the power to shuffle all
those committee members and even help *chairmen* keep
their jobs," said one of her black colleagues in the
House.

Clearly she was rising in power and influence in
Congress almost as quickly as she had in the Texas
Senate. It took time and work, but she was willing to
give them. Thus when, a few days after the opening of
the 94th Congress, she learned that the Houston police
department had a secret dossier on her, her first reaction was to wonder how law enforcement officials had

so much time that they could "intrude on the lives of public officials."

She was not the only prominent Houstonian on whom such a dossier had been kept. Others included the new mayor of Houston, Fred Hofheinz; fellow Congressman Bob Casey; several lawyers; a former member of the school board; prominent businessmen; and well-known fighters for civil liberties and the rights of the black community.

Barbara was not personally disturbed about her file. The idea that Houston police had wasted the time and effort to compile the dossier caused her to chuckle. But she was disturbed by this additional example of government disregard of individuals' right to privacy. "It is time, in my judgment, for the American government —state, local, and national—to get its own house in order and recognize that the civil liberties of the citizenry are to be protected at any cost," she said. Privately she wondered how in the world that could be done. The whole concept of civil liberties had been seriously eroded; disregard for them had spread like a cancer through all levels of government. She believed that the cure would have to begin with the highest levels, and she just did not feel the Republican administration was capable of policing itself. A real housecleaning was needed, and only an entirely new—in this case, Democratic—administration could do it.

Ironically, a month after the disclosure that Houston police had kept a file on her, Barbara Jordan received one of the highest honors the Texas Senate had ever given one of its former members. A specially commissioned portrait of her was unveiled, to be hung permanently beside portraits of Lyndon B. Johnson, the early state heroes, and of all people, Jefferson Davis, president of the old Confederacy.

Her former colleague in the Senate Chet Brooks said it was a shame Barbara's voice couldn't be captured in the portrait. "I may not talk openly from that portrait," she responded, "but when it stands there next to all of the august people we have ensconced on the walls of this chamber, it's going to talk."

To the large, mostly black audience who had come to witness the unveiling, she suggested, "Maybe you're here because you want to affirm the fact that in order for a portrait to hang on the walls of this chamber you do not need to be a former president of the United States or a warrior at the Alamo. You can be something else. You can be a person."

The majority of her audience knew exactly what she meant. She was referring to the fact that blacks traditionally had not been considered persons, in the full sense of the word, in America; and that even then, in the year 1975, there were whites who would deny "personhood" to blacks and other racial minorities. She returned to Washington to continue her efforts to gain real "personhood" for those to whom it was still denied.

The 1965 Voting Rights Act was scheduled to expire

in August, and Peter Rodino had introduced a bill that would simply extend it for another ten years. Barbara felt it should be broadened. The act had been designed originally to end voting discrimination against blacks in the South. It did not include southwestern states such as Texas, where a number of voting procedures that Barbara considered discriminatory continued. And it did not include racial or ethnic minorities other than blacks. Barbara introduced a bill that would extend the act to any area where less than 50 percent of eligible voters had registered in the 1972 presidential election and where printed election or registration materials were written only in English when more than 5 percent of the eligible voters had a mother tongue other than English. Under her bill the act would be broadened to include not only parts of the Southwest but also parts of the Northeast, and not only Hispanic-Americans but also French- and German-Americans. Two other Democratic representatives, Herman Badillo of New York and Edward Roybal of California, were sponsoring their own bills to broaden the 1965 Civil Rights Act. They differed from Barbara's mainly in their inclusion of parts of southern California and in not including any northeastern areas.

Immediately, many Texas officials protested. Conservatives of both parties were against what they saw as further federal intrusion into state affairs. Even some liberals felt that Texas was protecting its minority voters through state-imposed measures, without the need for federal intervention. One of those who felt that way was Democrat Jack Brooks, the other Texan on the House Judiciary Committee and a long-time proponent of civil rights measures.

Civil rights groups were also up in arms about the proposed changes in the act. Broadening it would weaken it, they charged. Or worse, the proposed changes might hinder extension of the bill in any form. They had an "understanding" with President Ford that he would support extension of the bill and they didn't want it threatened. The Black Congressional Caucus had included extension of the act to cover Spanish-speaking peoples among its announced legislative goals, but Barbara was the only one who was putting herself in the forefront of the controversy by introducing a bill for such inclusion.

Barbara was not being looked upon with much favor by black groups in March 1975. Earlier in the month she had resigned her seat on the Democratic Compliance Review Commission. She had been criticized for poor performance on the twenty-five-member body, which included six blacks. She had missed an important meeting on the party's affirmative action regulations, she had been late for a second meeting, and she had left before the final crucial vote that prevented the party's affirmative action policies from being extended to local units. Critics had charged that her close ties to white Texas Democrats, plus her ambitions for higher political office, were responsible for her poor performance. Barbara gave other reasons. Why did she leave the second meeting early? "The bickering became so enormous." At the beginning of March she said, "I am now reconsidering whether I should remain a member. I have to decide whether I have the time to spend on it." A week later she resigned, as did Deborah Renterria of Arizona. Barbara's resignation did not increase her stature in the eyes of the civil rights groups who opposed any broadening of the provisions of the 1965 Voting Rights Act. She was not, in their opinion, doing a very good job representing the interests of black people.

In this particular case it must be acknowledged that Barbara's critics had some grounds for complaint. Her performance on the Democratic Compliance Review Commission was a blot on her otherwise clean attendance record and commitment to duty. Certainly bickering is an irritating waste of time and Barbara is not the sort of person to endure it for very long. Still, missing that important vote was inexcusable. Perhaps she would have been better advised to resign earlier if she did not feel she could contribute sufficient time to the commission.

As to the criticism that her voting rights bill showed that she was not doing a good job representing the interests of black people, it is in the main unfair. Barbara had never promised to represent black people exclusively. She had promised to represent the people of her district and people all over the United States who had no voice in the decision-making processes that affect them. She intended to do just that. Realizing that the competing bills that she, Badillo, and Roybal had introduced could weaken the final goal at which all three aimed, she considered combining her bill with one of theirs. Renewal of the Voting Rights Act was being considered by a subcommittee of the House Judiciary Committee. Barbara was not on that subcommittee, but Herman Badillo was. Barbara and Badillo got together and at the end of March introduced a joint proposal to broaden the act. The new bill would cover less of California than the original Badillo bill and would not cover the areas of concentration of French- and German-speaking people that had been in Barbara's original bill. It was the sort of compromise for which Barbara had been criticized in the past, but she firmly believed the bill was necessary to protect the rights of the blacks in Texas and Hispanics throughout the United States. One day when she was testifying before the House Judiciary Committee in support of broadening the act, she pointed out that her own political career probably could have begun earlier if the act had been in effect in Texas in the early 1960s.

Republican committee member M. Caldwell Butler of Virginia started to make a comment. Barbara, who was a little tired of all the criticism she had been getting about her bill, sternly requested that Butler not interrupt her testimony. Later Butler apologized for the interruption, but added, "The observation I was trying to make was that if the act had been in effect earlier, you probably would be president by now."

As a second-term representative, Barbara was certainly far from the presidency, but at times it seemed that she was nearly as much in demand as a speaker. Early in May, as part of the required financial disclosures of members of Congress, she reported lecture fees of $12,500 from 1974 alone. And lectures for which she was paid constituted only a small portion of the number of appearances she actually made. There were speeches at Democratic fund-raising events and at testimonials for various friends and fellow members of the Texas delegation; there were awards and countless testimonial tributes to her. And she had received honorary degrees from numerous colleges and universities. Such unpaid appearances were part of her responsibilities as a public figure, and although they were time-consuming, Barbara generally did not mind them. They were usually pleasant and uneventful. In May 1975 she was invited to receive an honorary degree that she was particularly pleased to accept, since it was to be awarded to her by Texas Southern University at its annual graduation ceremonies.

Only later did Barbara learn that one graduate had been missing that day—Ovide Duncantell, who had stood in front of her office back in June 1972 and called upon her to pardon a jailed T.S.U. student while she was "Governor for a Day." Duncantell was to have received a bachelor's degree in sociology during the

ceremony, but instead he was in jail, having been
arrested for, among other things, resisting arrest,
felonious criminal mischief, public intoxication, dis-
orderly conduct, and jaywalking. Duncantell contended
that he had been arrested and jailed so that he could
not attend the T.S.U. graduation; that a "higher up"
had "thought it was an affront to colored people [for
Duncantell] to be in the same line with Barbara
Jordan." Barbara never learned whose side of the story
—Duncantell's or that of the police—was true.

Back in Washington Barbara actively went to work
on a bill that would abolish so-called fair-trade laws,
laws that were instituted during the Great Depression to
protect small businesses and small manufacturing concerns. What they amounted to were price-fixing laws
that were unfair to the consumer. Barbara had done
considerable research on these laws. She had found
that in states with fair-trade laws consumers paid up
to 37 percent more for products than persons in states
without fair-trade laws paid. Despite the fact that some
states had repealed their fair-trade laws, thirty-six still
maintained them. Barbara felt a federal law covering
all states would ensure balanced and fair enforcement.
In mid-May she introduced her bill into the House.
Because a similar bill had been introduced in the
Senate and because President Ford had indicated he
would support abolition of fair-trade laws, she did not
foresee any problem with the passage of her bill.

The bill to broaden the provisions of the Voting

Rights Act of 1965 was another matter. Back in Texas Governor Dolph Briscoe and other opponents of her bill were doing their utmost to prove that the Voting Rights Act did not need to be extended to Texas. In the middle of May Governor Briscoe signed into law a bill that required the use of bilingual materials in each election precinct in counties with more than 5 percent Hispanic population. In June he sent a letter to every member of the U.S. Senate stating that he bitterly resented congressional efforts to dictate Texas's election procedures. His and other Texans' attempts to forestall an expanded Voting Rights Act were fruitless, however. On July 27 the Senate passed and sent to the House a bill that would extend the act for seven years and expand its coverage to Texas and other areas with "language minorities." The House had already passed Barbara's bill, which called for a ten-year extension. But to resolve the differences between the two bills would require a House-Senate conference committee and before it could be reported out of the committee August 6 might pass and the 1965 bill would expire. No supporter of broadening the act wanted it to expire. On July 28 the House approved the Senate-passed bill by a 346 to 56 margin.

Barbara, who was the chief sponsor of the "language minorities" expansion, was invited to attend the ceremony on August 6 at which President Ford signed the bill into law. The president made brief remarks, which were printed out for him on large index cards. Barbara noticed the cards. After the signing, as the president chatted in the rose garden with members of Congress and civil rights leaders who had attended the ceremony, Barbara asked for the cards and wondered if he would autograph the last one for her. Ford obliged and Barbara smilingly put the cards into her purse.

Ordinarily Barbara was not a collector, but as she said, "This is my first big legislative victory," and she wanted the memento.

It is important to point out here just what is involved in getting a bill under the president's pen. In the House, as in the Senate, before a bill ever reaches the floor it must go to a standing committee, whichever one is appropriate to consider the particular bill. Once in committee it usually goes to a subcommittee, where it can be considered quickly or delayed indefinitely. A bill can languish in committee for years, but if its sponsor can get sufficient backing for it, he or she can usually get it moving. If the bill is recommended by the committee, it is reported onto the floor, where it is voted on by the full House. If it is passed, it must still be voted on by the Senate. If it is passed in the Senate, it goes to the president. If he does not veto it, the bill at last becomes law. Despite the length and complexity of this process, congressmen usually introduce or cosponsor many bills each session. One reason, of course, is that they must show their constituents that they are actively working for them and thus should be reelected. It is not unusual for an individual congressman

*Barbara Jordan with President Gerald Ford
and Congressional leaders*

to introduce between 200 and 500 bills in a two-year term. Barbara introduced or co-sponsored 72 bills during her first year in the House. But what really counts is getting one's bills passed, and Barbara had proved admirably that she could do that. During her first term she was the principal sponsor or co-sponsor of fifteen bills that became law.

In December she saw another bill for which she had been largely responsible signed into law—legislation to wipe out fair-trade laws. Barbara was invited to the signing ceremony, and had her photograph taken with Peter Rodino and President Ford and carried by the major news services. Although it is likely that she kept a copy of the photo, or at least a clipping from one of newspapers in which it appeared, Barbara needed no special mementos of the occasion. She felt like a veteran legislator by now.

There are some who think she *acted* like a veteran from the moment she arrived in Congress. "There was no learning process for Barbara Jordan," they say. "She seemed to know the day she got here how experienced congressmen act, how they get heard. She's unbelievably savvy politically—maybe it's Texas."

13 The Future for Barbara Jordan

Barbara's Texas-style initiation into politics had been very valuable, and when she reached Washington, D.C., being a representative from Texas certainly did not hurt. The Texas delegation was an extremely powerful group and had been so for a long time. Traditionally the Texas delegation had consisted almost exclusively of conservative Democrats, and there was power in such unity of political philosophy. Moreover, unlike U.S. legislators from urban areas, for whom a city judgeship was the ultimate goal, many of the Texans were former county judges from small, rural towns for whom a congressional seat was the highest goal they had ever hoped to reach. Having reached that goal, they stayed in Washington and gained seniority and maintained their cohesive force while other state delegations changed personnel frequently and amassed less seniority. The Texas delegation had achieved the height of its power in the 1950s, when Sam Rayburn was Speaker of the House and Lyndon B. Johnson was Senate majority leader. Through a combination of tenacity, traditional Texas-style political wheeling and dealing, and the financial support of the money interests back home, the Texans were the most formidable bloc in Congress.

By the time Barbara reached Washington, the power of the Texas club had begun to ebb. Congressional redistricting due to one-person–one-vote court decisions had eliminated some of the old rural districts, and new members elected from the big cities were often either Republicans or more liberal Democrats. The seniority system was beginning to come under fire, and some of the elderly Texans who were powerful committee chairmen were close to retirement. But in the 94th Congress Texans were still in control of nearly one third of the twenty-one standing committees of the House and of more than twelve subcommittees.

Just being from Texas, however, didn't automatically constitute acceptance in the Texas club. Acceptance from its older, powerful members had to be earned, and Barbara had done it in a remarkably short time. She understood their politics and proved quickly that she knew just as much as they did, if not more, about oil depletion allowances and cotton prices and the Dallas money market, as well as civil rights law and the provisions of the Equal Rights Amendment. What's more, she fit in well with them, didn't assert either her blackness or her femaleness, didn't make them feel uncomfortable. Once accepted, she became a "card-carrying member" of the club. In addition to attending the weekly meetings of the delegation, she had lunch with them, made contacts through them, sounded them out on issues. Her approach has always been to "seek out the power points," and there is no more powerful group in the House.

As stated before, her close association with the otherwise white, male Texas delegation has given rise to criticism from those who feel she should be more conspicuously on the side of issues directly affecting blacks and women. Very soon after she arrived in Washington, she made clear her feelings that the Congressional Black Causus should concentrate on legislation rather than on taking public, general positions. "There are bills which come up and which affect black people directly," she says, "and in my judgment the Black Caucus ought to be looking for those pieces of legislation and seeing to it that amendments are offered which would change the impact if that impact would be negative or adverse to black people. I have told my Black Caucus colleagues that we cannot be the Urban League, the N.A.A.C.P., the Urban Coalition, the

Afro-Americans for Black Unity, all rolled into one. We have a commonality of issue—blackness—but we cannot do what the other organizations have been designed to do through the years."

She attends meetings of the House women's group only when she has time. She makes a firm distinction between working and "crusading." Recurring throughout her career have been the charges that she is a "sellout" to white, conservative interests. She prefers the word "compromise" to "sellout." "I think compromise is necessary," she says. "I don't call it cutting deals with people: I call it trying to get done what I need to get done and making necessary compromises which do not violate principles in getting those things done. I think it's necessary in political life." Barbara also points out that she has never sold out her constituents on legislative issues and that there is nothing wrong in dealing with those who are powerful if you get enough in return.

She is almost religiously responsible about her job, working twelve to fourteen hours a day, spending far more than the average time on the House floor, and being present for a remarkable percentage of roll-call votes. Adam Clayton Powell, Jr., used to complain about the number of roll-call votes taken in the House:

"There are men in Congress who have never contributed anything to the advancement of our nation, but sit all day on the floor of Congress, just to look around and see whether two hundred and eighteen members are present," he said in his autobiography. "If not, they question the presence of a quorum. Then the Speaker makes a count, finds there is no quorum, and three bells are rung. One must then scurry over to answer the roll call."

Barbara may complain privately about the number of roll-call votes that are taken in the House, but she does not question them publicly. Her record of roll-call vote participation is well over 90 percent.

As she walks back and forth between the House floor and her office, or between her office and her various committee rooms, she rarely speaks to those she passes, even if she knows them. Most of the time she is so absorbed in thought that she doesn't notice them. She rarely enters the Washington social scene, preferring to make her contacts over lunch, for example, rather than over cocktails or at an evening reception of some sort. Because of this behavior, she has acquired a reputation for coldness and aloofness.

Barbara can indeed be cold. She is well-known for her sarcasm, such as her comment to a congressman who was regaling the Texas delegation about the high price of fertilizer one day. After listening to him for a time, she grew tired of his long-windedness. "Congressman," she said, fixing her piercing eyes on him, "it's refreshing to hear you talking about something you're really deep into."

Barbara's administrative assistant, Rufus Myers, says: "Some people misunderstand her because they're so used to dealing with people who are not entirely serious when they're on the job. She just feels that when she is on the Hill taking care of the people's business, she doesn't have time to try and please everybody by being what they might call 'nice.' She just wants everybody to state their business as briefly as possible so that she can have enough time to do her job. It's really as simple as that."

She is decidedly not a favorite interview subject for reporters, especially for those assigned to do a personal story on her. Many an interviewer's questions are prefaced with phrases like "I've been warned not to ask you about . . . ."

"I can't remember being more apprehensive about an interview with a public figure than I was before (and, occasionally, during) my talk with her," wrote veteran newswoman Meg Greenfield. "The message is conveyed in her every word and gesture: Don't tread on me. And she is also known for a certain brusqueness associated with another minority group to which she belongs: that of very smart people who see the point long before others have finished making it and who have a low threshold for muzzy argument or political blah."

Barbara is indeed very smart, but she is not a smart aleck. Her fellow representative from Texas and friend Charles Wilson explains: "Now, Barbara doesn't try to play possum on you; she doesn't mind letting you know that she's got a very, very high I.Q. But she doesn't embarrass you by making you feel that you're nowhere close to being as smart as she is. It's an amazing thing how she can be standing there schooling you about something and still make you feel that you knew all that right along. Not all smart people can do that; some of them love to make you feel right ignorant."

Certainly, there are some who do not particularly like Barbara. There are others who like her as a person very much but disagree with her politics. But there seems to be no one who does not respect her, and in Washington respect counts almost more than anything else. Some would argue that influence is most important, but a major component of influence is respect. Other components of influence are contacts, intelligence, and the ability to get things done. Barbara has all of them, and something more. Charles Wilson tries to explain it:

"It's that along with her superior intelligence and legislative skill she also has a certain *moral authority* and a—it's just presence, and it all comes together in a way that sort of grabs you, maybe you're kind of intimidated by it, and you have to listen when she speaks and you feel you must try and do what she wants. . . . It's something you really can't describe."

That indescribable "something" has made Barbara Jordan, after only a very few years in Congress, one of its most influential members. In February 1975 she was the subject of a front-page profile in the *Wall Street*

Journal (no small honor in itself), which stated that she had achieved "more honor and perhaps more power than most members . . . can look forward to in a lifetime." In some ways, the characteristics that could very well have been strikes against her—her color, her sex, and her southwestern origins—have worked for her. We are in an age when all three of these characteristics, formerly scorned and discriminated against in politics, are now at a premium. At least on the surface, attempts are being made to give blacks, women, and southerners a greater voice in the political process, and Barbara Jordan happens to represent all three groups.

Barbara was chosen as one of the two keynote speakers at the Democratic National Convention held in New York City in July 1976. The other was a white male, former astronaut, and congressman from Ohio, John Glenn. Barbara, a black female, was a logical choice to provide balance. But she was chosen for other reasons. Race and sex aside, she had become one of the most prominent Democrats in the country. It turned out to be a very wise choice, for Barbara's address was the highlight of the first evening and one of the highlights of the entire convention. After a colorless and unmemorable speech by John Glenn, Barbara was introduced, and she took her place at the podium amid a standing ovation. The huge Madison Square Garden thundered with applause. She waved one hand, and the audience cheered. She raised both hands and they cheered louder and stomped their feet in delight. Smiling, she waited for the tumult to subside. Then she began:

"One hundred and forty-four years ago, members of the Democratic Party first met in convention to select a presidential candidate. Since that time Democrats have continued to convene once every four years and draft a party platform and nominate a presidential candidate. And our meeting this week is a continuation of that tradition.

"But there is something different about tonight. There is something special about tonight. What is different? What is special? I, Barbara Jordan, am a keynote speaker."

She was interrupted by wild applause and cheering, and she would be interrupted again and again as she spoke of the problems of the country and her hopes for America. It was an impressive speech, impressively delivered in her sonorous, almost hypnotic voice; and when she finished, she received a thunderous and standing ovation. The overwhelming response was one of pride, not just from women because she was a woman, not just from blacks because she was black, not just from Democrats or from Texans, but from all segments of the population, because she was an American. There were tears in the eyes of many of her listeners, both at the convention and at home, and for others the breathless, almost light-headed feeling that comes after a profoundly moving experience.

Above: *Barbara Jordan responds to applause before beginning her keynote address at the 1976 Democratic Convention.* Below: *Ms. Jordan leaves a meeting with President-elect Jimmy Carter in December, 1976.*

A week later, on the floor of the House of Representatives, Charles Wilson moved that Barbara's keynote address be reprinted in the Congressional Record. "I would guess there are few Republicans in the House who did not watch Ms. Jordan deliver this speech in New York," he said, "and fewer still who did not share our pride in our colleague. Many have said so. . . . We Democrats in the House proved our regard and respect for the egalitarian procedures of our great convention. *We sent the best we had.*"

James Earl Carter won the Democratic presidential nomination at that convention against token opposition, and though he faced a hard fight against Republican incumbent Gerald Ford, he was certain he would win the election. Barbara Jordan was also optimistic. A combination of black, northern liberal, and southern white votes could give the nation its first southern-born president since Zachary Taylor, and she looked forward to election day.

There were blacks who were not as strongly behind Jimmy Carter. Shirley Chisholm, congresswoman from New York, and Representative Parren J. Mitchell of the District of Columbia, to name two, were concerned about Carter's so-called "fuzziness" on issues and about his southern origins. They pointed to his conservative positions when he ran for the Georgia governorship in 1970 and to the fact that he had received only 7 percent of the black vote in that gubernatorial election. During his primary campaign in 1970 he had visited a private academy that had a whites-only policy, and though the stated purpose of his visit was to reassure Georgians of his support for private education, the implication was that he supported school segregation. In 1972 he had praised a resolution by the Georgia legislature that called upon Congress to pass a constitutional amendment banning school busing, and in the same year he brought pressure to bear on Democrats in Congress to weaken the Voting Rights Act of 1972. Based on such a record, these blacks were hesitant to believe in Carter's avowed liberalism and concern with black people.

It will be noticed, however, that the black leaders who voiced these misgivings were nearly all non-southerners. Among southern black leaders only Georgia state representative Julian Bond refused to support Carter. The others found it possible to support him quite energetically despite his rather flawed past record on civil rights.

Being southerners themselves, they understood the kind of atmosphere in which Jimmy Carter had reached political maturity. His seeming fuzziness on the issues was not so much a matter of having no firm policies as it was of the kind of campaign style to which he and other southerners were accustomed. Barbara Jordan may always have run issue-oriented campaigns, but most southern candidates run now, as they have always done, personality-oriented campaigns. The new breed of southern politicians tries to project what has been called a "best man" image, emphasizing trust and integrity and basic decency more than concrete issues. That was the kind of campaign Jimmy Carter was running for the presidency.

Barbara also did not worry about Carter's past civil rights record. Things had been changing quickly in southern politics over the past few years, and what a white southern politician said or did in 1970 or 1972 often had little connection with what he said or did in 1976. Many strident segregationists a decade earlier were openly wooing the black vote now. As a politician, she felt, Carter had a right to change his views on issues just like anyone else. And finally there was that subtle understanding between southern blacks and whites that neither northern whites nor northern blacks could comprehend—a sense of knowing where one stood with the other without the shadows of false liberalism to obscure the truth—the shared pride in the South that the election of a southern-born president could do so much to bolster.

In November it was just that coalition of blacks, southern whites, and northern white liberals, that carried the election for Jimmy Carter, and of the three groups the black vote constituted the most solid bloc. Carter received well over 90 percent of the black vote nationwide. Black votes made the difference in Mississippi and Louisiana. In Texas, Barbara Jordan's home state, Carter won the state's bloc of twenty-six electoral votes by some 150,000, but blacks provided 276,000 votes. No wonder Jimmy Carter has called the Voting Rights Act of 1965 the most important political event of his lifetime; it could also be called the most important single event affecting his own political career.

There was no question that Jimmy Carter owed a lot to the blacks who had voted for him, and it was expected that he would reward his black supporters with important government jobs. He intended to have a racially and sexually representative Cabinet, he said, and naturally, soon after the election speculation was rampant about whom he would choose. The name of Andrew J. Young, congressman from Georgia and Carter's staunchest black supporter, was on every list of potential black cabinet members; and so, on many of these lists, was the name of Barbara Jordan. Perhaps she would be chosen as secretary of housing and urban development or secretary of labor. But time passed and the cabinet appointments were made, and though Andrew Young was named ambassador to the United Nations, Barbara Jordan received no appointment.

Had she been asked? Had she turned them down? Neither the Carter people nor Barbara would say. It was rumored that she had indeed been approached with regard to a cabinet post and had responded negatively, or rather, that she had informed the Carter transition team that she would only be able to accept the post for two years. Senatorial elections were coming up in 1978, and according to Washington scuttlebutt, Barbara Jordan was going to run for a Senate seat.

Barbara would neither confirm nor deny these rumors, but as more information was leaked or said to be leaked about her consideration for a cabinet post, she felt constrained to set the record straight. In April, after the President had made all his major cabinet selections, she explained in an interview with Barbara Walters what had really happened.

She had received a call from Carter back in December. He had asked her if she would be interested in "exploratory talks" with him about a position in his administration, and she had agreed to meet with him. "Anybody would talk to the President-elect," she told Walters. "I'm not *that* 'cold and aloof,'" she added, referring to her reputation. By the time she went to Blair House, the mansion across the street from the White House in which Carter and his transition team had set up operations, she had decided the only position she would even consider would be that of Attorney General. The President-elect asked for a first, second and third choice, but she had only one, and in a brief but friendly meeting she told him so.

Carter chose longtime friend and associate Griffin Bell as Attorney General, and the appointment was confirmed by Congress despite objections from some civil rights groups on his civil rights record.

Asked why she thought she had not been chosen, Barbara answered, "Well, let me state the obvious. Mr. Carter was and is entitled to his own choice, and his choice was not Barbara Jordan. Now that should end the matter. As to why I would think the chances were remote to begin with, bringing the 'baggage' which I have always had to carry from birth—not always a heavy baggage, sometimes light, but the black, woman thing—it is conceivable that some in the South would have considered an appointment of *me* to the position of attorney general as a real slap in the face. I don't know that such was the case, but I certainly suspect it could have entered into the consideration."

It has been suggested, at various times and by various people, that Barbara, who has already chalked up a long string of firsts, might well be the first black/female vice-president, the first black/female president, the first black/female Speaker of the House, the first black/female attorney general, the first black/female governor of Texas, the first female member of the Supreme Court, not to mention the first black senator from the South. Publicly she has always encouraged such speculation. Back in July 1972, when she served in the honorary position of "Governor for a Day," she stated that she might someday want to retain the governor's chair a little longer. During a spring 1976 program of *Meet the Press*, when she was asked if the country was ready for a woman, particularly a black woman, as a vice-presidential candidate, she smiled and answered, "The country is not ready, but it's getting ready, and I'll try to help it."

But Barbara is a stone realist and she is aware that there are limits to her possibilities. Privately, and in moments of particular candor with reporters, she alludes to those limits. She knows it would be very difficult for her to win a statewide election in Texas. When one reporter pointed out in 1972 that Frances "Sissy" Farenthold had gotten 45 percent of the vote in that spring's Democratic gubernatorial primary, Barbara gave the reporter her well-known, baleful glare. "Sissy's white," she said impatiently. "It still does make a difference, you know."

In the same year, newly elected as the first southern black female representative, she was asked about her future. In return she sarcastically posed another question: "Where would I go from here?"

Barbara's realism derives from solid bases. She has not forgotten how hard it was to be elected to the Texas legislature or how much time it took Texas to integrate its public schools. The newspaper reports of bombings of black homes in New York suburban neighborhoods or demonstrations in South Boston against busing do not escape her keen eyes. Also, being a politician *par excellence,* she is aware that conventional political wisdom holds that whenever the question of race comes up, it must be assumed that the American electorate is primarily made up of closet segregationists.

Though the political possibilities for blacks in the South have advanced light years forward from what they were a decade ago, they are still not wide open or boundless. The elective positions held by southern blacks are mostly at low levels. Only one southern black has been elected by statewide vote, Joseph Hatchett, who won a place on the Florida Supreme Court. In the fall of 1976 Howard Lee, a black former mayor of Chapel Hill, North Carolina, got 46 percent of the vote in a Democratic primary runoff for lieutenant governor, but it was not enough to win. One of the few blacks in the Mississippi state legislature, Fred Banks, Jr., says: "It may take twenty years to get a black elected to statewide office here."

Despite these limiting factors, Barbara Jordan will probably not remain simply a representative from Texas. She aspires to, and will presumably achieve, higher political office. It is likely that whatever higher office she does achieve will be an appointive one, such as attorney general or Supreme Court justice, or if it is an elective one, it will be an office for which people who know and have worked with her will vote, like Speaker of the House. Senator Jordan? Vice-President Jordan? President Jordan? To paraphrase the point Representative Caldwell Butler once made, Barbara was probably born too early to achieve such positions.

That is the pragmatic view. But American politics is a curious blend of pragmatism and idealism. There is still room in America for strange and unusual happenings, for "rags to riches" stories, for a poor black girl from Houston's Fifth Ward to fulfill her dreams, whatever they may be.

Perhaps, as the United States begins its second two hundred years, its people can put aside their prejudices against sex and race in the face of the undeniable intellect and charisma of a woman like Barbara Jordan. To do so would be a testimonial to our maturity as a people, a proof to the rest of the world that a "made-up" country of many nationalities can really work, and a fitting way to greet the new era.

Appendix

Legislative Accomplishments
of Representative Barbara Jordan

94th Congress [1975–1976]

Member, House Judiciary Committee
    Member, Subcommittee on Monopolies and Commercial Law
    Member, Subcommittee on Administrative Law and Governmental Relations
Member, House Committee on Government Operations
    Member, Subcommittee on Intergovernmental Relations and Human Resources
    Member, Subcommittee on Manpower and Housing
Member, House Democratic Steering and Policy Committee
Member, Speaker's Task Force on Legislative Program for the 94th Congress

Member, Speaker's Task Force on House Recommendations
to the Democratic Platform Committee
Principal sponsor of H.R. 3247, to extend and expand the
Voting Rights Act of 1965; P.L. 94-73
Principal sponsor of H.R. 2384, to repeal federal authoriza-
tion for state "Fair-Trade" laws; P.L. 94-145
Principal sponsor of H.R. 8557, a private bill for the relief
of Carmen Thomas, P.L. 94-88
Principal sponsor of strengthened civil rights enforcement
procedures for the General Revenue Sharing Program
Principal sponsor of strengthened civil rights enforcement
procedures for the Law Enforcement Assistance Ad-
ministration
Co-sponsor of the following bills which have become law:
Prohibiting the president from increasing the price of
food stamps and eliminating many from eligibility;
P.L. 94-4
Providing for low-income workers a tax credit on
Social Security taxes; P.L. 94-12
Emergency Housing Act, passed in revised form; P.L.
94-50
Health programs extension; P.L. 94-63
Allowing women to enter military academies; P.L. 94-
106
Allowing Government Accounting Office to collect and
analyze energy situation reports from oil companies;
P.L. 94-163
National Women's Conference; P.L. 94-167
Prohibiting military intervention in Angola; P.L. 94-
212

Opening meetings of federal agencies to the public; P.L. 94-409

Authorizing state attorneys general to bring antitrust suits on behalf of the citizens of their states; P.L. 94-435

Providing increased antitrust investigative powers for the Justice Department; P.L. 94-435

Requiring large corporate mergers to be reviewed by the Justice Department for antitrust purposes; P.L. 94-435

Creating an Office of Inspector General in the Department of Health, Education, and Welfare to investigate fraud and program abuse

93rd Congress [1973–1974]

Member, House Judiciary Committee
Member, Subcommittee on Monopolies and Commercial Law
Member, Subcommittee on Claims

In July 1974, the House Judiciary Committee voted to recommend to the House of Representatives that Articles of Impeachment be exhibited in the Senate against Richard M. Nixon, president of the United States; the impeachment vote was the culmination of an eight-month investigation

On November 29, 1973, the House Judiciary Committee voted to recommend the confirmation of Representative Gerald R. Ford as vice-president of the United States

On December 12, 1974, the House Judiciary Committee voted to recommend the confirmation of Governor Nelson A. Rockefeller as vice-president of the United States

Member, House Democratic Committee on Organization and Review

In October, 1974, the House passed the so-called "Hansen Committee" recommended reforms of the Rules of the House of Representatives including reorganization of the jurisdiction of the standing committees of the House

Principal sponsor of civil rights amendments to Law Enforcement Assistance Administration authorization; P.L. 93-83

Co-sponsor of the following bills which have become law:

Amendments to the Older Americans Act; P.L. 93-29

Ban U.S. involvement in the war in Indochina, incorporated into the 1973 Supplemental Appropriations bill; P.L. 93-50

Requiring congressional approval before sending further troops abroad, incorporated into the State Department Authorization; P.L. 93-126; and the War Powers Act; P.L. 93-140

American Revolution Bicentennial Administration; P.L. 93-179

Home Rule for the District of Columbia; P.L. 93-198

Child Development and Abuse Prevention Act; P.L. 93-247

National Insurance Against Catastrophic Natural Disasters; P.L. 93-288

Mandating continued use of food commodities for school lunch and child nutrition; P.L. 93-326

Requiring congressional approval prior to the impoundment of funds incorporated into the Budget and Impoundment Control Act; P.L. 93-344

Legal Services Corporation; P.L. 93-355

Youth Conservation Corps; P.L. 93-408

Right of Conscience in Abortion Procedures Act, incorporated into Public Health Service Act extension; P.L. 93-435

Establishing the Big Thicket National Preserve; P.L. 93-439

Making illegal sex discrimination in the granting of credit, incorporated into the Equal Credit Opportunity Act; P.L. 93-495

Assuring the free flow of information to the public, incorporated into the Freedom of Information Act Amendments; P.L. 93-502

Emergency Public Service Jobs created; P.L. 93-567

Assuring freedom of emigration from the U.S.S.R., incorporated into the Trade Reform Act; P.L. 93-618

Community Services Administration, creation and operations; P.L. 93-644

Providing for expanded social services to the poor; P.L. 93-647

Bibliography

Books

Barone, Michael, et al. *The Almanac of American Politics, 1976.* New York: E. P. Dutton & Co., 1975.

Benton, Wilbourne E. *Texas: Its Government and Politics.* Englewood Cliffs, N.J.: Prentice-Hall, 1976.

Chamberlain, Hope. *A Minority of Members: Women in the United States Congress.* New York: Praeger, 1973.

Hearings of the Committee on the Judiciary, House of Representatives, Pursuant to H. Res. 803. Washington, D.C.: U.S. Government Printing Office, 1974.

Katz, Harvey. *Shadow on the Alamo.* Garden City, N.Y.: Doubleday & Co., 1972.

McComb, David G. *Houston: The Bayou City*. Austin: University of Texas Press, 1969.

Morris, Willie, ed. *The South Today*. New York: Harper & Row, Publishers, 1965.

Report of the Committee on the Judiciary, House of Representatives, Impeachment of Richard M. Nixon, President of the United States. Washington, D.C.: U.S. Government Printing Office, 1974.

Rice, Lawrence D. *The Negro in Texas, 1874–1900*. Baton Rouge: Louisiana State University Press, 1971.

Young, Margaret B. *Black American Leaders*. New York: Franklin Watts, 1969.

Magazine Articles

"A Sight for the Eyes of Texas," *Newsweek*, May 22, 1972, pp. 34–35.

"Barbara Jordan—Rising Political Star," *U.S. News & World Report*, February 9, 1976, pp. 43–44.

"Jimmy Carter: Peanut Farmer to President?" *Encore*, April 5, 1976, pp. 18–21.

Jordan, Barbara. "How I Got There: Staying Power," *Atlantic*, March 1975, pp. 38–39.

Jordan, Vernon. "Blacks Have a Claim on Carter," *Newsweek*, November 22, 1976, p. 15.

"Jordan: Seeking the Power Points," *Newsweek*, November 4, 1974, p. 22.

Levine, Jo Ann. "Impact in Congress," *Christian Science Monitor*, March 18, 1974, p. 6.

Lomax, Louie E. "Women Lawmakers on the Move," *Ebony*, October 1972, pp. 48–56.

"Out of a Cocoon," *Time*, September 27, 1976, pp. 40–42.

Phillips, B. J. "Recognizing the Gentleladies of the Judiciary Committee," *Ms.*, November 1974, pp. 70–73.

Sanders, Charles L. "Barbara Jordan: Texan Is a New Power on Capitol Hill," *Ebony*, February 1975, pp. 136–142.

Newspapers

Austin *American-Statesman*, 1966–1976.

Chicago *Daily News*, October 24, 1975.

Houston *Chronicle*, 1962–1976.

Indianapolis *Recorder*, June 19, 1976.

New York *Times*, 1971–1977.

San Antonio *Express & News*, 1966–1976.

Washington *Post*, October 22, 1972, July 27, 1974.

Wall Street Journal, February 1975.

Ephemera

Current Biography, 1974, pp. 186–189, 189–192.

Speeches made by Barbara Jordan.

Photographs appear courtesy of:
The Houston Post, 85, 102, 112, 121, 135
Johnson Publishing Company, 28
United Press International, frontispiece, 5, 57, 154, 179
Wide World Photos, 41, 72, 190

Index

About the Author

James Haskins is the author of more than twenty books for adults and young adults. His recent titles include *Fighting Shirley Chisholm*; *Adam Clayton Powell*: *Portrait of a Marching Black*; *A Piece of the Power*: *Four Black Mayors* (all Dial); *A Most Reluctant Hero*: *Ralph Bunche*; *The Story of Stevie Wonder*; and *Witchcraft, Mysticism and Magic in the Black World*.

Mr. Haskins is a member of the faculty of the graduate school of education at Manhattanville College and a professor in the experimental college at Staten Island Community College. He lives in New York City.